The Lost Children

Carolyn Cohagan

Aladdin

NEW YORK LONDON TORONTO SYDNEY

ALADDIN

An imprint of Simon & Schuster Children's Publishing Division
1230 Avenue of the Americas, New York, NY 10020
First Aladdin hardcover edition February 2010
Copyright © 2010 by Carolyn Cohagan

All rights reserved, including the right of reproduction
in whole or in part in any form.

ALADDIN is a trademark of Simon & Schuster, Inc., and related logo
is a registered trademark of Simon & Schuster, Inc.

For information about special discounts for bulk purchases,
please contact Simon & Schuster Special Sales
at 1-866-506-1949 or business@simonandschuster.com.

The Simon & Schuster Speakers Bureau can bring authors to your live event.
For more information or to book an event contact the Simon & Schuster Speakers
Bureau at 1-866-248-3049 or visit our website at www.simonspeakers.com.

Designed by Jessica Handelman
The text of this book was set in Berkeley Oldstyle Book.
Manufactured in the United States of America
0610 FFG
2 4 6 8 10 9 7 5 3

Library of Congress Cataloging-in-Publication Data
Cohagan, Carolyn.
The lost children / Carolyn Cohagan.
p. cm.
Summary: When twelve-year-old Josephine falls through a wormhole
in her garden shed into another time and place, she realizes the troubles
she has at home are minor compared to what she has to tackle now in the
world where she has landed.
ISBN 978-1-4169-8616-4 (hc)
[1. Time travel—Fiction. 2. Voyages and travels—Fiction.
3. Friendship—Fiction. 4. Family problems—Fiction.] I. Title.
PZ7.C65948Jo 2010
[Fic]—dc22
2009016608
ISBN 978-1-4169-9054-3 (eBook)

For my parents,
who never made me get a real job

There are so many people that supported and nurtured this book that I cannot possibly list them all here. I am forever indebted to Emily Klein, for always being such a willing reader and champion of my work; my writers group, for urging me to keep writing prose; my manager Eddie Gamarra, for his patience; Rick Richter, for being so open; my editor, Liesa Abrams, for jumping on board so enthusiastically; and Joe Conway, for his consistently great notes. In addition I want to thank Sarah Aubrey, Elisa Roth, Kristen Roberts, Vanessa Scorso, David Russell, Celia Purcell, Lou Denton, and Sue Booth-Forbes and her invaluable gift of the Anam Cara Artist's Retreat.

ONE

Josephine Russing owned 387 pairs of gloves. She had them in wool and cotton and silk. She had them in plaid and paisley and print. She even had a pair that had been made from the fur of an albino sloth.

Josephine, her gloves, and her father, Leopold Russing, lived in a big empty farmhouse miles and miles away from the nearest neighbor or trading post. Josephine had no friends to speak of, but even if she had, she would never have invited them to visit her home. Other children might expect her father to say hello, to ask their names, or to serve them iced lemonade. And when he didn't, they might learn Josephine's *most* horrible, *most* shameful, *most* unspoken secret.

Her father ignored her completely.

Mr. Russing skulked around their house in silence,

reading, cooking meals, or washing clothes, occasion-
ally glancing at Josephine as if she were a neighbor's cat
who'd sneaked in the window. Since her mother had
died, Josephine's only indication that her father remembered she existed was that each week he brought her a
new pair of gloves. He never said anything about them, or
acknowledged when she wore them, but every Friday evening when Josephine checked her chest of drawers, there
would be a brand-new pair of gloves inside. Josephine
would have preferred a conversation or the occasional
"How was school today?" but she wore the gloves duti-
fully, accepting each new pair as some minute sign that
her father actually cared for her.

But it was hard to believe that Mr. Russing cared
for anything. He was an imposing presence, tall with
salt-and-pepper hair that he slicked back, exposing an
intimidating widow's peak. His brown eyes were inscru-
table and never seemed to rest on anything for long.
Josephine was fairly certain he couldn't name her eye
color (amber) or her age (twelve). He wore expensive
suits that were always perfectly pressed, along with his
own special pair of gray silk gloves.

He was extremely unpopular in the town, and it wasn't
just because he was strangely quiet and wore the expression of someone who'd just smelled sour milk. People
hated him because he was responsible for the most outra-

geous law ever to be passed in the town's history: *Every* citizen was required to wear gloves at *all* times.

This might be fine if one was a banker or an accountant or something of that sort, but imagine what it was like for the farmers and carpenters and bakers, who worked with their hands. They *hated* the law, but if they were caught not wearing gloves, they were fined.

How did this silly law get passed in the first place? It happened one night many years ago when Mr. Russing was in the middle of a heated game of five-card stud with the city mayor. Mayor Supton had four jacks and was feeling a bit cocky. But Leo Russing had a straight flush, and when he won, he decided to forgo his monetary winnings and demand that the mayor pass a new law on his behalf. The mayor quickly acquiesced, happy to escape with his wallet intact.

Mr. Russing was the only man who manufactured gloves in the town, so one can imagine how much this law improved his business. He had three factories lined up in a row like ducks—that is to say, they were actually shaped like ducks (Josephine's father had bought the buildings from a man in the bathtub toy business who was down on his luck). In one building the gloves were designed. In another they were cut and pinned. And in the third they were sewn, by hand, by women who'd been shipped over from an island across the ocean and who didn't mind sewing gloves . . . while wearing gloves.

He was the wealthiest man in town. And people hated him, for his money and for his stupid law. And the children hated Josephine. As they sat in the classroom, hands sweating and itching from their gloves, they would glare at her and whisper mean things. But she was too shy to defend herself, to try to explain that she had nothing to do with the gloves and that she hated wearing them too.

Josephine barely remembered her mother, and the recollection was less of a picture and more of a sensation, an ethereal feeling that Josephine couldn't pinpoint but that most children know very well. It was a sense of safety and love. For Josephine this feeling was elusive, as if she were sopping wet and couldn't remember what it was to be dry.

Surprisingly, the vision from her early childhood that haunted Josephine the most was not of her mother, but of her father. She could recollect him standing on the front lawn, his hair a rich brown, smiling and waving to her mother inside the house. He was, as always, wearing a crisp suit and the gray gloves, but he was smiling and— Josephine was just sure of it—he was happy. It was very difficult to reconcile the joyful man on the lawn with the father she now lived with. But she clung to the memory desperately, only letting it out at night when she could sink into it like a warm duvet.

Josephine had always gone to school of her own accord. Her father didn't notice if she went or not, which many children might imagine as an ideal situation, but not Josephine. She loved books. And school was the only place where she could get her hands on more, so she attended regularly and worked diligently. She felt confident when she was reading. She imagined that because she was able to admire and understand the characters in the stories, the characters (had they been real) would have liked and understood her in return. Sometimes when she neared the end of a story, she would force herself to read *very*, *very* slowly, because she dreaded the moment when it was all over, when she would have to look up and remember her own dull life. So she always read the last paragraph twice before turning the page, detesting that brutally blank final sheet.

Josephine had a delicate heart-shaped face, a button nose, and long eyelashes that made her eyes wide and bright. Not that anyone saw her eyes, since she always walked around with a curly mop of hair obscuring her face. She was lean and gangly, and she hated her spindly legs.

While the children would have nothing to do with Josephine, she intrigued the schoolteacher, Ms. Kirdle.

Josephine possessed an almost frightening ability to remember lectures word for word, and unlike the other children, Josephine never talked to her neighbors, or giggled when Ms. Kirdle's new shoes squeaked, or pointed if she saw a dog out the window. She always sat still and captivated at the back of the classroom, chewing on her frizzy locks.

And she got perfect marks.

Ms. Kirdle, a kind woman with mannish eyebrows, worried about Josephine's apparent lack of friends. When she told the children to form groups, no one wanted to include Josephine. Ms. Kirdle only had to look down at her own gloved hands to understand their resentment, but she still thought they were being unfair. She sometimes managed to slip Josephine extra books when no one was watching.

Every afternoon school ended with Ms. Kirdle reading aloud from a story, and this was Josephine's favorite part of the day. She would close her eyes and listen to Ms. Kirdle's dulcet voice, temporarily forgetting that eventually she would have to gather her books and papers and return to her unbearably quiet house.

But that callous bell would always ring, jolting Josephine out of her reverie, and the room would fill with the sharp scratchings of chairs on the wood floor as the other children hurried to escape. And Josephine would watch out the window as mothers came to gather their broods, retie unlaced shoes, and patiently listen to the ceaseless list of wonders and complaints that school always produced. Only after the other children and mothers had walked away would Josephine leave the building. She preferred not to hear the whispering her presence seemed to provoke among adults.

This was Josephine's life—school, books, and a weekly pair of new gloves—until one spring day when a small boy named Fargus arrived in her garden.

TWO

It was a hot, humid day, and as Josephine walked the dusty three miles home, she was in a bit of a snit. Ms. Kirdle had been lecturing all week about horticulture and had ordered all of the students to go home and plant tomatoes. Josephine was annoyed because when she got home, she'd been planning to finish a delightful book about a giant who falls in love with a barn. And now she would have to deal with these vexing tomatoes instead.

She wearily walked in her front door and hung her schoolbag on a peg in the hall closet. She took off her gloves, a purple pair with feathers at the cuffs (sometimes she walked around bare-handed before her father got home). She removed a small sack of seeds from her pocket and carefully read the directions. She saw there were certain tools she was going to need for the job.

She sighed, for the tools were located in Josephine's least favorite place in the entire world.

Old and rickety, the toolshed at the back of their property seemed to be held together by its abundant cobwebs, and whenever Josephine was required to go inside it, she had the distinct feeling that something had just ended, that moments before her hand had landed on the door latch, there had been a party of rats, a meeting of roaches, or a small union of spiders conspiring to land in her hair.

She shuddered at the thought and begrudgingly put on her mud boots, an old pair that had once belonged to her father, and went out the back door to the patio. She awkwardly plodded in the oversize shoes across the vast lawn to the small shed at the back. Josephine's house had been built just after she was born, but this shed had been around for generations. It belonged to a time that Josephine couldn't even picture, and if she tried to imagine the people who had lived then or the many people who may have stood in front of the shed just as she did now, it made her teeth hurt (Josephine's molars frequently ached when she tried to process difficult or abstract information).

She lifted and pulled at the squeaky door until it relented with a burst of stale air. Even in the afternoon sun, the shed was dark and cool, like a mausoleum. She entered slowly and instinctively ran her hand through her curls, searching for spiders. As soon as Josephine's eyes had adjusted to the darkness, she could see the small shovel and watering can she needed. She snatched them up and darted out of the shed. As the door swung shut behind her, she almost thought she heard an exhale, as if the shed were relieved to see her go.

Back in the daylight, she surveyed the backyard for an appropriately sunny place for her tomatoes. She saw a dirt patch that was near enough to the house that she could spot it from the kitchen window but far enough away not to annoy her father.

She walked briskly across the lawn toward the chosen sight and heard a crunch beneath her foot. She lifted her shoe and saw that she had stepped on a snail. Her heart sank as she thought of his long, deliberate journey across her yard, and she imagined the mama snail and baby snail who would be waiting for him to return. But he never would, thanks to her thoughtlessness. She wistfully cleaned off her boot and reminded herself to watch her step.

She was soon hacking at soil with the little shovel, turning the earth as Ms. Kirdle had shown them. She reviewed the teacher's lecture in her mind.

"The tomato is a 'perennial,' which means it grows year-round. The plant grows as a series of branching stems, with

buds at the tips that do the actual growing. It needs plenty
of water and six hours of sunlight a day."

Josephine opened her little packet of seeds and
poured them into the fresh hole.

She wished the teacher had asked them to grow
something more interesting, like maybe a nice cactus.
A cactus was a *succulent*, which was a word Josephine
liked a lot, and she said it out loud now: "Ssssucculent."
It had something called a taproot that grew underground
and stored energy for the cactus to use if there was a
drought. Some of them could go as long as *two years*
without water. And just in case her father should decide
he didn't want anything growing in his lawn, a cactus
had needles to protect itself. A tomato was just silly and
squashy and completely helpless.

She covered her tomato seeds with plenty of water,
as Ms. Kirdle had instructed. As she packed the soil
back into the hole, she began to converse out loud.
Josephine had been talking to herself for years but
often didn't realize it. Most of the time, since she had
no one else to talk to, she would tell her father about
her day.

"Johnny Baskin's been wearing the same socks
to school for weeks and he's starting to smell. Nelly
Wipshill likes Brian Union but Brian likes Fiona Valley."

She would imagine him nodding his head and

laughing, as he had done that day when her mother had still been alive.

A twig snapped to Josephine's right. She looked over, expecting to see a robin or a squirrel. But what she saw made her cry out. A small, barefoot boy with a suitcase in his hand was standing on the lawn, staring at her. He was an intense boy with hard brown eyes and small lips. Josephine caught her breath.

"You scared me to death!" she scolded him.

He continued to stare at her without answering.

"What are you doing here?" Josephine asked, squinting at him from behind her tangle of hair. There was something very strange about this boy.

He took a step toward her and put the suitcase down on the ground. He was a few years younger than Josephine. She couldn't imagine why he would be wandering around alone all the way out here. "Are you lost?" She tried a smile.

He twisted his face and opened his mouth as if to respond, but no words emerged. Just air.

"I'm Josephine. What's your name?" she demanded. But still nothing.

Josephine stood up, brushed herself off, and walked past the boy to the front of the house. He followed her like a loyal puppy. She looked up and down the dirt road, expecting to see his mother or father. But the road was empty. The next house was miles away. Was he some sort of runaway? She'd never seen him in school or anywhere else in town. She didn't know what to do. She turned back toward the boy and for the first time noticed that he wasn't wearing gloves. *Definitely not local*, she thought. He was scrawny and pale and looked as if he hadn't had a good meal in a long while.

"Do you want some food?" she tried.

He smiled and nodded, so Josephine led him back to the house. They entered the kitchen and Josephine took off her mud boots. She pointed to a chair at the table. It was the one she usually used. Somehow she felt that if the boy sat in her father's chair, her father would know about it immediately. Almost as if he had read her thoughts, the boy put down his suitcase and used *it* for a chair.

Josephine retrieved some leftover oatmeal from the refrigerator and began to reheat it on the stove. She added plenty of brown sugar and milk, the way she liked it herself, and set it down in front of the boy. He stared at it for a long moment and then stuck his nose deep into the bowl for a sniff. When he brought his head back up, he had oatmeal on his nose. Josephine giggled and the boy self-consciously wiped his nose on his sleeve and went back to staring at the oatmeal.

Finally, as if a switch had been thrown, he grabbed the spoon and began wolfing down his food, shoving it in so fast that Josephine was afraid he would choke. He finished the oatmeal in seconds and then used his fingers to gather the sugar that was left on the sides of the bowl. He licked them, ecstatic, as though he'd never tasted anything sweet before.

"You were hungry, huh?" Josephine asked.

He looked at her, more alert now, eyes shining. He nodded.

"How did you get here?"

The boy looked away from her, at the ceiling and then the floor.

Sensing his anxiety, she added, "I won't tell anyone. I promise." She looked intently at him and he stared back, long and hard. It seemed to Josephine that he was trying to make up his mind about something. Then, in one motion, he got up from his suitcase and walked out the back door.

"Hey!" She rushed after him onto the patio. He was standing there, pointing, as tense as a rabbit near a wolf. She followed his finger, and when she saw what he was pointing at, she sucked in her breath.

"That's where you come from?"

The boy nodded solemnly.

Josephine suddenly felt cold despite the sweltering sun. The boy was pointing at the shed.

THREE

After a moment of silence Josephine seemed to wake up. "You mean, that's where you were hiding?" The boy shook his head. "You live *there*? In our shed?" He shook his head again: *No.* Josephine studied him, searching for signs of oddness. Perhaps he was slow or had been hit over the head with a shoe. His poor parents were probably out searching for him in the gloomy rain. She glanced up at the bright sun. In all the books she had ever read, if your child was missing, it was always during a gloomy rain. She looked back at the boy and he was staring at her again, his eyes big and questioning, as if he wanted something from her. There was something familiar about his piercing stare, but she couldn't quite . . .

She had an idea. "Do you want me to read you a story?" Josephine always found it so comforting when

Ms. Kirdle read aloud to the class; she thought maybe this boy would like it too.

He shrugged and Josephine decided he'd shown adequate enthusiasm. She led him back inside, her mind racing with the various titles she might choose. Should she read him some sort of adventure story with horses? (Josephine loved horses, although she'd never had the pleasure of riding one.) Or something less scary, like a love story? She really didn't know what boys liked, since she'd never talked to one.

The boy clunked up the stairs behind her, and Josephine was keenly aware of how irritating her father would have found the brutish noise of his feet.

They entered her bedroom and she scanned the many bookshelves for her favorite books. The boy looked around the room with his mouth open. By his expression, Josephine wasn't sure if he had ever seen a book before. She finally chose a short story about sailors and mermaids.

"You sit on the bed and I'll sit over here," she told him. She took her place in a rocking chair that had once belonged to her mother. The boy climbed happily onto Josephine's feather bed, almost sinking out of view.

Josephine delicately opened the book and began to read in a voice similar to the one Ms. Kirdle used, calm and slightly mysterious. "Once upon a time, there was a sailor called Simian Swallow, and although he was a sailor, he was afraid of water. . . ."

The boy listened closely, his eyes shining. But by page ten, when Simian was fighting the Mermen of the Outer Depths, the boy's eyelids were starting to droop. And by page fifteen, he was fast asleep. Josephine was so caught up in the story, she didn't notice until he started gently snoring.

She quietly closed the book, marking their place, and watched the boy sleep. She wanted to help this boy, to keep feeding him and reading him stories, to teach him how to talk, even. If this boy didn't have a family, then where would he go? Her house was plenty big. He could live with her and then they could play together, like she had seen other children do at school. They could play hide-and-go-seek and tag-you're-it. They could walk to school together and share secrets. They would be brother and sister and best friends. Josephine's heart trembled at the thought.

The problem, of course, was Josephine's father. Mr. Russing wouldn't want anything to do with a strange child, an urchin wearing no shoes or gloves who couldn't speak. Josephine imagined her father swatting the boy away with a rolled-up newspaper. And why would he want another child around when he didn't even want the one he had? Josephine's mind swam with ideas. Maybe she could hide the boy temporarily, at least until she came up with a good way to approach her father.

Yes, I must hide him until I have a plan.

She knew her father would walk through the door that night at precisely ten after six, as he did every night. She left her room, went downstairs, and checked the clock in the kitchen. She had five minutes until her father arrived. She ran back up the stairs to tell the boy about her plan.

"I've had a wonderful idea—," but before she could finish the sentence, she realized that the boy was gone. He was no longer in the bed where she had left him, and he didn't appear to be anywhere else in the room. "Hello?" she called. "Where have you gone?"

She ran back down the stairs, but he wasn't in the kitchen or the living room. "Hello . . . little boy?" She felt foolish for not knowing his name.

She opened the front door, looked up and down the street, and saw dust rising where a figure was approaching. Her father!

It then occurred to Josephine that perhaps the boy had gone into her father's bedroom upstairs. If her father found him there . . .

She had only a minute until Mr. Russing arrived.

She took the stairs two at a time, running so fast she

developed a stitch in her side, panic rising into her chest as she tried to imagine what her father would do if he found the boy. She herself was forbidden to go inside Mr. Russing's room and she was terrified that the boy had decided to hide there. She opened the door and peeked inside. The bedroom was the same stark, stale place it had always been.

At that moment, she heard Mr. Russing entering the front door downstairs. He cleared his throat, his version of "I'm home." Luckily, he expected no response from her. She took a deep breath, darted into his bedroom, and checked the closet and under the bed. She looked out the window to the backyard, to see if perhaps the boy had returned there, but it was the same empty expanse of green it always was. Josephine felt a bit frantic. She turned around and gasped as she saw her father standing in the doorway.

The sight of him instantly reminded her that she was not wearing gloves. "I'm sorry, Father. I took them off just—" He turned and walked away before she could finish. She closed her mouth and followed him out of the room, his unspoken disapproval stinging her worse than thundering admonishments. She went to her bedroom and grabbed a pair of gloves from the drawer, brown and gray tweed.

Then she stiffly marched down to the kitchen and

prepared the quickest dinner she could muster, a soup made from leftovers.

As she stirred the spontaneous stew, she considered the boy and what could have happened to him. She had left him alone only for a moment and their house was surrounded by dry, flat land that concealed nothing. How could he have gotten away so quickly? The only logical explanation was that the boy was hiding in the shed. It was such an obvious answer that she felt foolish for running so frantically around the house.

She threw open a cabinet, grabbed a bowl and spoon, and poured a thick serving of soup. She listened to make sure her father wasn't approaching and then dashed out the back door. She crossed the lawn, the sloshing soup threatening to spill onto her gloves.

When she reached the shed, she carefully placed the bowl and spoon next to the door. She didn't have time to check inside. She knocked on the door and then sprinted back to the kitchen, entering seconds before her father did. She immediately began pouring the remaining soup into bowls for their meal.

Dinner, as always, was a silent affair, but there was a new tension in the air. Josephine dared not look toward the shed, petrified that she would give away her secret. But she also avoided looking at her father directly, worried that if she looked him in the eyes, somehow he would be able to read her mind and would know all about the boy.

She gulped down her soup, mentally willing her father to finish as well. After what seemed like a lifetime, he finally put down his spoon and wiped his mouth with his napkin. Josephine felt her body begin to relax, but when Mr. Russing stood to leave the table, his foot caught on something. He raised an eyebrow, grunted "Hmmff?," reached down, and pulled up a small leather suitcase from under the table.

Josephine sucked in her breath.

He began to examine the case more closely. Josephine, frozen in fear, waited to see if he would open it. She couldn't imagine what it contained. Clothes? Schoolbooks? A wash towel? In her worst nightmare she saw her father opening the suitcase to find dozens of bats that would swarm the kitchen and poke out his eyes. She couldn't explain where this dark vision came from—she just knew he mustn't open the case.

She stood up from the table. "That's mine, Father. I left it under the table by accident."

He looked at her, suspicious.

"I'll just go put it in my room, where it belongs." She reached out and, with some force, pried the case from his grasp. She scampered from the kitchen and was halfway to the stairs when she heard an unfamiliar baritone. "Josephine . . ."

She froze. She couldn't remember the last time she had heard her father's voice. She was torn between her urgency to get upstairs with the suitcase and the desire to stay and hear what her father wanted to say.

"Yes, Father?"

There followed a long, painful pause.

"Nothing," he mumbled.

Nothing. As usual. The momentous occasion of him speaking to her had resulted in "nothing." She sighed and trudged up the stairs to her bedroom, locking her door.

She sat on the floor and placed the suitcase in front of her. It was a plain brown case that had seen a lot of wear. There were no labels or tags to suggest to whom it belonged. She unlatched the rusty clasp and, with trepidation, opened the lid.

She blinked in surprise, for the suitcase was, after all this trouble, completely empty.

She was utterly confused. She had felt down to her marrow that something would be inside, something that would explain the small boy and their strange time together. And downstairs she had felt a deep sense of foreboding, as if her life had depended on her father's not knowing the contents of this case. How could she have been so wrong?

The inside of the top of the case had a large pocket, where one usually expects to find loose change and old train tickets. She ran her hand along the inside of the pocket and was about to laugh at herself for such dramatic behavior when her finger touched the edge of something that felt like a playing card. She brought it out and saw that it was a worn photograph. She looked at it and suddenly felt dizzy, as if a hundred mosquitoes were trapped inside her head.

The picture was of *her*, standing in a summer dress in a strange garden. This was a photograph that to any outsider would not have been alarming, but it made Josephine feel as if a tiny nail had just been tapped into her heart. For in the photograph a large family surrounded her. She was flanked by brothers and sisters, the boys sporting the same lopsided grin as Josephine, the girls cursed with the same chaotic mess of hair.

In the photograph a proud father stood on the left, as far in spirit from Mr. Russing as an oak tree from a stinging nettle. And then next to the father stood a smiling woman holding a kicking baby. A mother. And Josephine knew as certainly as she had ever known anything in her life: *This family belongs to me.*

FOUR

The next day Josephine awoke and got ready for school like any other day. She brushed her teeth and washed her face, and she thought about brushing her hair. But when she looked at her huge straggly mane in the mirror, she decided there was no time. She changed into a plain white top, brown pants, and a pair of gloves so shiny that they almost seemed metallic. Josephine had no idea what they were made from, but they reminded her of the inside of an oyster.

Her father was dressed and out the door at 7:33, as he was every day, and as soon as he was out of sight, Josephine stopped getting ready for school. She had no intention of going today. Instead, she ran to the kitchen, grabbed the remains of a lemon cake, and wrapped it in wax paper. She then took off her walking shoes and got her rubber boots from the hall closet.

It was a cool morning and the leaves on the trees struggled against the wind. She stepped onto the back patio and stared at the shed. It looked harmless enough from here. The air was cool and electric, and she sensed a storm about to break. She had a brief moment of concern for her newly planted tomato seeds, but they could wait.

She trudged ungracefully to the shed and grasped the latch. For a moment it wouldn't budge, and Josephine thought it had been locked from the inside. But as soon as the thought formed in her mind, the latch gave way and she found herself opening the door. The shed was darker than usual due to the overcast sky, and Josephine squinted in order to see all the way to the back. But she couldn't. It was like . . . what? A word popped into her head, a word she'd recently learned in school: *abyss*. It was like an abyss.

"Hello?" she asked in a timid voice. She scolded herself for her meekness and tried again. "Are you in there? I've brought you cake."

She stepped inside, and suddenly the door swung shut behind her. Blinded by the darkness, she put a hand out in front of her, afraid she might step on a rake. She willed herself forward, her breath heavy and loud in the stillness as she forced one foot in front of the other, trying not to think about spiders and snakes. Her outreached hand suddenly hit cold stone and she knew she'd reached the far end. There was no one in the shed.

Josephine felt a rush of sadness and, then, just as quickly, she felt a bit silly. How could she have believed that someone was living in her shed? Surely she was too old for such fantasies. She leaned against the stone, taking comfort in its coolness. Her eyes began to adjust to the dark and then something on the ground caught her eye—something shiny. She squatted and saw it was a spoon, and next to it sat the soup bowl that Josephine had left outside the night before. It was empty.

So the boy had been here! She smiled, knowing that her new friend was near.

Suddenly, the door to the shed flew open and a violent wind came barreling through the entire room. Josephine's eyes and lungs were assaulted by dust and she began to cough, waiting for the wind to calm, but it refused. It just grew stronger and stronger until it seemed a small cyclone was inside the shed. Josephine covered her eyes and struggled toward the door, but the wind was so strong that she couldn't progress forward.

A pot of soil smashed into the wall beside her, and a coiled rope unwound and came thrashing across Josephine's thighs like a vicious snake. She yelled for help but knew it was futile. Her father was miles away.

Just when Josephine felt it couldn't get any worse, a

spade scraped its way across the middle shelf, turned its sharp edge toward her, and then flew at her head. She screamed and threw herself against the back wall, waiting for the spade to impale her. There was a flash of light, an explosive *crack*, and suddenly Josephine's body tore through the back wall of the shed as if it were paper!

She plunged backward expecting to hit the ground, but her body kept falling. She saw nothing but blackness around her. She kicked her legs and waved her arms, but her hands had nothing to grab on to. She yelled, but there was no sound. Had the spade hit her? Was she dead? She felt icy cold, and she was terrified she was going to descend forever. Just then her body slammed onto something hard and solid. Her last thought before she passed out was *I hope I didn't drop the cake.*

FIVE

When Josephine awoke, she felt a throbbing ache in her head. She was disoriented, but she knew she was lying on her back. She lifted each leg, one at a time, to make sure they still worked and bent her arms to and fro. Then she twisted her neck, first to the left and then to the right. Nothing seemed broken. She rolled over and soon forgot the pain, for she realized she was lying in an unfamiliar storage cellar. It was an enormous room made of heavy stones, with wood piled in one corner and bags of flour and salt stacked in another. There were wooden barrels full of who-knows-what pushed against one wall and a narrow slit of a window near the ceiling. It let in a paltry amount of light, and shadows, ominous and shifting, peered at her from every nook and cranny.

She had never seen this place before. Maybe she was

still asleep and this was a dream? Or could this possibly be part of the shed, some level below the ground that she never knew existed?

She pressed her hands onto the cold floor. She stood, her head pulsating with pain and confusion. And she truly began to panic as she realized that this was not a dream and that she was most definitely not in her shed.

There was a stairway on the far wall that led to a door. She crept toward it, relieved to find that her legs still seemed to function. She advanced up the stairs and then heard voices emerging from behind the door. She was comforted. Surely she could find someone who would explain where she was.

She reached for the doorknob but froze. One of the voices was barking orders. So instead of opening the door, she pressed her ear against it and strained to listen.

"No, no, that's all wrong! You're cutting them too thick. Start over. . . . If you let that soup boil over, I'll be using *your* bones for stock tomorrow. . . . Ida, if I see you lick your fingers again, I'm going to throw you down those cellar stairs!"

The cellar? Josephine nervously backed away from the door, but it didn't open. So she pressed her ear back onto the wood and tried to hear more. She felt desperate to know where she was, but this woman sounded frightening and awful. The voice began to screech.

"That's it, Ida, you ant-brained speck of fly dung! Into the cellar!"

Heavy steps crossed the room and a child started to protest. "But I—"

Josephine scurried down the stairs and looked around, panicked, for a place to hide. At the last moment, she crouched behind the sacks of flour and salt. She heard the door open at the top of the stairs and the shrieking voice seemed to fill every pore in Josephine's skin. "I hope you stole your share of food, Ida, because you won't be eating again today!"

Josephine heard what sounded like someone being shoved down the stairs, tumbling and thudding, and the door slammed shut. She sat frozen in her hiding place, afraid to make a sound. There was some shuffling and Josephine imagined she was hearing the child stand up. Then the girl started to whistle. It was a happy song and reminded Josephine of something her mother might have sung.

Ida, if Josephine heard correctly, began strolling around the room. She soon neared the sacks of flour and salt. Josephine held her breath because, from what she could hear, the girl was starting to climb the pile of sacks. But her weight proved too much, and the sacks began to fall toward Josephine, who looked up just in time to see a bag of salt careening toward her head. She blocked it with an elbow, and as she did, she made a sound like *"Oooaaf."*

The whistling stopped, and Josephine knew at once that the girl had heard her. There was nowhere to run, so she raised herself to full height and adopted her meanest face, gritting her teeth and bugging out her eyes. A second later, the girl came around the pile and discovered Josephine, ready to attack.

Much to Josephine's embarrassment, the girl laughed.

She was about Josephine's age, but smaller and thinner, and although there were dark circles under her eyes, she was still striking, with cropped black hair and sharp green eyes. She wore plain cotton clothes she had probably outgrown last spring and no gloves. Her face had an adult quality that Josephine found intimidating.

Finally, the girl stopped giggling and said, "You're Josephine."

Josephine was shocked. "Yes . . . but how do you know?"

"Fargus told me all about you."

"Fargus? I don't know anyone called Fargus."

The girl looked at Josephine as if she were as dumb as twigs. "Of course you do. You gave him oatmeal and salty soup."

"Oh. He never told me his name." Ignoring the dig at her cooking, Josephine was happy to hear news of her friend. She extricated herself from her shoddy hiding place and approached the girl.

"Well, that's no surprise. I'm Ida, by the way."

"Nice to meet you."

"Fargus is gonna be so mad! He thinks he's the only one who can find you, and I sure showed him! Ha!" Ida perched herself on top of some fallen sacks. "You look different than I thought you would."

Josephine looked down at herself. Her once-white shirt was now covered in dirt, and she knew her hair must have been bigger than a garden shrub. Her enormous rubber boots felt absurd, but when she looked back up, Ida was staring at her shiny gloves.

"Why are you wearing those?" she asked bluntly.

Since Ida didn't know about the mandatory glove law, Josephine surmised she was no longer in her town. She took off the gloves, shoved them into her pocket, and changed the subject.

"Where am I?"

"You don't know?" Ida crinkled her nose.

"No. I have no idea."

"Wow. I wish *I* could forget where I was."

"I didn't forget," she said, frustrated that this bossy little girl seemed to have no sympathy for her plight. "I've never been here before."

Ida tilted her head. "Lucky you." She raised her

arms in a dramatic gesture. "Then I welcome you to the Higgins Institute for Wayward Children and Forsaken Youth, or as I like to call it, the Forsaken Institute for Unwanted Children and Wayward Lice."

"Who's that horrible woman who threw you down the stairs?"

"That's Kitchen Maggie. And she's not so bad. It's Stairway Ruth you've got to look out for. She'll beat you for burping." Ida whispered conspiratorially, "As far as me and Fargus know, she has *never* gone to the bathroom. Isn't that *bizarre*?" She jumped off her flour sack and began to pound a closed fist against her palm. "Kitchen Maggie's as dense as a rolling pin, easy to play, you know? *She* thinks she's punishing me but *I* think I just got out of kitchen duty."

Ida then raised both fists, shuffled her feet, and began punching one of the flour sacks, like the boxers Josephine had read about in the paper. Ida smacked the bag with all her might. Josephine had never seen a girl hit anything before, and she was mesmerized.

"We have to find a good hiding place for you. Maggie will pop an eyeball if she finds you here."

"I really just want to get home—"

Ida stopped punching. She was getting winded. "You can't leave! Not before Fargus sees you. He'll never believe me otherwise!"

Fargus. Josephine really did want to see him. "Okay, then. How about I say hello to Fargus and then you show me the way home?"

"The way home?"

"The way that Fargus came to see me."

Ida was suddenly annoyed. "I don't know how to get there. I thought *you* did."

"No. It was an accident! I don't even know what I did. I was trying to find Fargus and he told me—I mean he *showed* me—that he'd been hiding in the shed. . . ."

"That's just swell," Ida said, her voice dripping with sarcasm. "I can't believe Fargus thought we should live with you."

"He did?" Josephine couldn't help but smile.

"But the plan was for us to come to *you*, not the other way around," Ida criticized.

"I'd like that, really. But I don't even know how to get outside."

"Oh, you don't want to go outside," Ida said, then spit on the floor. Josephine felt a bit repulsed but didn't say anything. "The Brothers would just catch you."

"The Brothers? Who are the Brothers?"

Ida stared at Josephine and pushed her black hair away from her eyes. "You don't know? You really are strange. The Brothers are—"

A sound at the top of the stairs made them both look up.

Someone was opening the door.

"Hide. Now!" Ida ordered.

Josephine dropped to the ground and scurried behind the sacks. She peered through a small opening and saw Kitchen Maggie enter with a scowl. "Don't get happy, Ida. I just need more flour." She was enormous, with flabby pale skin, stubby arms, and an apron as big as a sheet. The first thing that came to Josephine's mind was *sea cow*.

And the sea cow was headed straight for Josephine's hiding place!

Ida, determined to stop her, made a quick tear at the top of a flour sack and then hit it as hard as she could. A giant *poof* of white powder covered Ida from head to toe, making her look like a giant chicken about to be deep-fried. Josephine would have laughed if she wasn't so terrified.

Kitchen Maggie spun around, eyes blazing. She walked toward Ida, her beefy fists clenched, and stopped only inches from Ida's small frame. She glared down at her. "Do you know how much flour's worth, you miserable piece of snot!?" She looked as if she was about to strike the girl, when a monstrous grin formed on her blubbery face. "This is your lucky day, Ida. You get to visit Stairway Ruth." She grabbed Ida's arm and pulled her up the staircase, leaving a trail of flour behind.

Josephine could see the dread on Ida's face as Maggie shoved her toward the kitchen. Then the door slammed shut and Josephine was alone once more.

She had no idea what to do now. She had so many more questions for Ida. *Why am I here? What happened to my house? Who are the Brothers? Who can I ask for help?*

She decided that it was best to stay hidden for now, so she curled into a tight ball and lay among the flour sacks, her heart pounding, her mouth dry.

What would happen to Ida? Whatever her punishment, it would be Josephine's fault.

She didn't know how long she'd been in the cellar, but she knew that she would never get home before her father returned from work and he would be furious. Or maybe he wouldn't even notice. Which would be worse? She put her head down and began to cry.

SIX

About an hour passed without any sign of Ida, Fargus, or Kitchen Maggie. Her tears had stopped but Josephine's legs were starting to cramp. She decided to risk leaving her hiding place. The light coming through the slitted window was fading and Josephine feared she didn't have long until the entire cellar was thrown into blackness.

She started to examine the walls, feeling every crack and irregularity, searching for a door or a hole. She didn't really know what she was looking for. It was as if she had appeared in this cellar out of thin air.

She was hungry. She thought sadly of the lemon cake, but it was nowhere to be found. She needed water. As her stomach began to rumble, she couldn't help but consider the kitchen at the top of the stairs.

Surely Kitchen Maggie was in bed by now and Josephine could help herself to a glass of milk.

And she wanted to find Fargus and Ida. She was frightened on her own. She wondered how many children lived in this institute and if they were friendly. Anxiety churned in her chest. For the first time ever, she wished her father were with her. Even his silent presence would have been better than this.

A sound from the top of the stairs made her jump. She scampered over to the woodpile, but she knew she wouldn't make it in time. The door opened, and a thick beam of light caught Josephine in midcrawl.

"I told you she was here." It was Ida. Josephine felt herself begin to breathe again. Ida was at the top of the stairs, smugly standing next to Fargus. "Why are you crawling on the floor?"

Josephine stood up, embarrassed. "I thought you were Kitchen Maggie."

"Oh, she went to bed ages ago. And Stairway Ruth doesn't start patrolling until midnight." Ida marched down the stairs, while Fargus stayed up at the top, as shy as ever. He looked exactly the same as when he had been at Josephine's house. He wore the same pants and shirt and remained barefoot.

"Hi, Fargus." Josephine smiled up at him. He grinned back, pleased, it seemed, that she remembered him. "Ida told me your name." He stared at her for a moment, and then crept down the stairs.

Josephine remembered that she'd been crying and wiped her cheeks with the back of her hand. "Did you get in terrible trouble?" she asked Ida.

"Nah," Ida answered, pride in her voice. She grabbed a pipe hanging from the ceiling and began to swing on it. "They took away my meals for tomorrow, but Fargus will sneak me his, won't you, Fargus?"

Fargus nodded at her.

Josephine was bursting to ask her next question. "Fargus, how did you get into my shed?"

Fargus opened his mouth but said nothing. Like the first time he'd met her, he pushed out a bit of air that contained no sound—and that was it.

Instead, Ida answered. "He can't tell you anything. Fargus can't speak." She jumped down, a pleased expression on her face.

Fargus suddenly ran for Ida and kicked her in the shin.

"Ow! You little flea magnet, that hurt!" Ida rubbed her leg. "I was just being honest. If I'm wrong, then why don't you say something, toad breath?" Fargus stared at her, defiant and ready to strike again, but then, just as quickly, he deflated like a balloon and dropped his eyes to the floor.

Ida spoke to Josephine in an exasperated tone. "Fargus has a temper. He thinks he's Mr. Tough."

Josephine put her hand on his shoulder. "It's okay, Fargus. My father never speaks. I'm used to it." Fargus stuck his tongue out at Ida and then beamed at Josephine.

"We'd better get going." Ida stood impatiently at the foot of the stairs.

"What?" Josephine asked, panicking. "You just got here. Please don't leave me alone again!" She felt as if she couldn't breathe.

"We have to, or Stairway Ruth will see we're out of bed."

"What am I supposed to do? I can't stay here all night by myself!" She thought of the door shutting once more, the thick darkness surrounding her, the coldness of the cellar floor. Her hands shook at the idea.

"Fargus thinks he can get back to your house, but it will take him a while to find the way, so we have to wait until morning to try it."

"Really?" Josephine smiled hopefully at Fargus. "Is that true, Fargus?"

He hesitated a moment, then nodded.

Josephine stepped to him and hugged him, relieved. When she released him, she said, "The morning? I guess I'll be okay until then." But deep inside she wasn't so sure.

Ida turned to leave. "Good. Let's go, Fargus. Hurry."

And then the two of them tiptoed up the stairs, opened the door, and were gone.

Josephine loathed being alone again, and she dreaded the night that lay ahead, but at least she knew she would be going home soon. The thought of her room and her books gave her some relief, along with a bit of new bravery. Her stomach was knotted up in hunger. Surely it would take just two seconds to grab a little food from the kitchen?

SEVEN

Stairway Ruth was on evening patrol. There wasn't much point these days with so few orphans left in the Institute, but Ruth was a staunch believer in routine. Every night at precisely midnight she grabbed her favorite lashing stick (which she thought made a particularly satisfying snap when it landed on the back of a child's legs) and started her rounds of the building. She began with the sleeping quarters in the east wing, to make sure the children were in their beds. And then she moved downstairs to check the dining hall, the library, and the classrooms. Next, through the kitchen and up to the meat storage tower. She had done it for so many years, she could do it with her eyes closed.

Unlike Kitchen Maggie, Ruth was lean. Her pointy joints only seemed capable of moving at extreme angles. Children near her were always worried about getting an elbow in the eye or a knee in the back. When confronted with the pursed face of Stairway Ruth, orphans tended to tremble, cry, pee their pants, or all of the above. And Ruth cherished their fear—she fed off it.

She had just finished a sweep of the classrooms and was approaching the kitchen when she heard a noise—a scraping. *Screet screet.* She stopped cold and listened carefully. She heard it again. It was coming from the kitchen! Ruth's heart leaped with joy. One of the little brats was most certainly trying to steal extra food, and she was going to catch him or her red-handed! Ruth savored these moments like most people savored a juicy roast.

On tiptoe, she approached the door to the kitchen, her lashing stick high above her head, ready to come crashing down on the tiny unsuspecting head of one of the children. She violently kicked open the door.

"Drop it, cockroach!" she cackled.

Josephine froze in terror, a meat pie halfway in her mouth.

Ruth was so shocked by the appearance of a new child that for a moment she didn't move.

Taking advantage of Ruth's surprise, Josephine leaped for the door. But Ruth came to her senses, threw her body in front of her, and yelled, "Maggie! Intruder!" She lunged to the wall and pulled a red lever. A deafening bell began to ring. *CLANG! CLANG! CLANG!*

Ruth reached for Josephine, but the girl plopped to the ground and scurried under the kitchen table. Ruth raised her lashing stick and began sweeping it underneath the tabletop. It flicked Josephine on the arm and she cried out in pain. *"Ach!"*

Kitchen Maggie came bursting through the door. Her hair was wrapped around red curlers, and her huge mushy body was flimsily covered in a polka-dot nightgown. Ruth pointed under the table. "Under there!" Maggie knelt down and growled. From Josephine's perspective, a huge terrifying beach ball was trying to eat her.

She jerked away, but Ruth was waiting and nabbed her from behind, dragging her across the floor and then onto her feet.

Josephine struggled like a trapped butterfly. "Let me go!" she squealed.

"What's this? Where did she come from?" Maggie asked.

Ruth smiled. "Must be some runaway who broke in here to find food. The Master will be very pleased. I'd say you and I just got us a freebie!"

Maggie looked Josephine up and down while the girl glared back, ready to kick or bite if she had the opportunity. "Isn't she a queer one? That's some strange costume she's got on."

"Look at this rat's nest on top of her head," Ruth replied. "We might need to shave it off. Can't have lice running around the place."

Josephine bucked again, trying to get free. "Don't you touch me!" she screamed, but Ruth's grip was like a vise.

Maggie leered, showing several missing teeth. "Where should we put her?"

"I think a few nights in the meat room will take the edge off her. The stink in that place would make a soldier beg to go back to war."

"No, please!" Josephine pleaded. "I just want to go home!"

Maggie laughed. She walked over to the red lever on the wall and pulled it back up, shutting off the alarm bell. Leaning into Josephine's petrified face, she said, "But don't you go messing with my meat, or we'll have *you* for dinner instead!"

Maggie, satisfied that Ruth had everything under control, shuffled back to bed smirking, leaving Ruth to drag Josephine to a narrow door with a large bolt. She slid open the lock, threw open the door, and shoved Josephine inside. "Start climbing!"

"My father has money. He can—"

"Start moving, or you'll feel my stick again," Ruth threatened.

Josephine saw spiral stairs leading up and up into pitch-blackness. She felt tears burning her eyes, but she didn't want to give Stairway Ruth the satisfaction of seeing her cry. So she steeled herself and walked up into the darkness.

The stairway was narrow, and she needed to place one hand on the wall to keep her balance. If she slowed down at all, she felt Ruth's stick in her back. After a minute or so, she reached a door at the top. It, too, had a bolt. Ruth reached roughly around Josephine, sliding the bolt to the right and pushing open the door.

Josephine was hit by the smell of something sharp and rank. The room was pitch dark, and although she couldn't see anything, she could tell it pulsated with life.

"Get going." Ruth shoved her forward and Josephine fell and landed on the floor, her hands skidding in a sticky, unknown substance. "Happy dreams!" Ruth screeched as she shut the door and bolted Josephine inside.

Josephine sat there a moment, perfectly still, as she assessed the space around her. The smell was so strong and horrible that she cupped her hands around her nose, only to find that her hands smelled even worse. She was shaky and her mind was spinning, but she had the terrifying sensation that the walls around her were breathing.

"Hello?" she asked. "Is someone here?"

Suddenly, sounds bombarded her—a mad rustling, and then, *twit twit*, echoing over and over. They were familiar sounds, not particularly frightening, but she couldn't place them. Her fear was blocking her senses, and she felt that if only her heart could stop beating so intensely, she would be able to hear better.

The noise dissipated somewhere above her, so she knew the ceiling was high. The sound reminded her a bit of passing the tearoom near the schoolhouse, where all the ladies gathered to gossip. Yes, it was like a group of old ladies tittering at the latest scandal. Josephine clenched her fists and willed her eyes to adjust to the darkness.

She began to make out a small square opening on one wall. She walked toward it and found a deep window, more than a foot thick, with no glass. She stood on tiptoes, hoping to see something, *anything*, but could make out nothing except black night. A small amount of fresh air blew in, and she greedily gulped at it, trying to relieve herself from the drowning odor.

She was still thinking of the old women back home and how they would end up gossiping about her strange disappearance, standing at their picket fences, nattering away like chickens. *Chickens!* she thought. *That's it! That's the sound. No, not quite . . . More like . . .* She turned around and focused on the shapes in the dark. "Pigeons!"

As her eyes adjusted, she saw that pigeons were sitting in hundreds of individual nooks carved out of the stone wall, and they continued up for at least two stories. Josephine was filled with relief and then embarrassment at having been so scared. Of course it was pigeons. Now the sound could be nothing else. There were feathers everywhere, and pigeon dung was the smell violating her nose. She looked at her hands in disgust and found some feathers to wipe them on.

Now that her fear had lessened a bit, she wanted to understand what Ruth had meant by "meat room." Back home, a meat room was a cold, dry place where one used salt to dry out different game. Her father bought their meat from a shop in town, so they didn't have that kind of room. And why would anyone want to eat pigeons? *"Blllech,"* she said aloud, sick at the thought of the meat pies she'd just eaten in the kitchen. Had they been made of minced pigeons?

She looked back at the strange open window and realized that the opening was just large enough for a pigeon to fly through. *Ah,* Josephine thought, beginning to understand. She'd once read that pigeons always returned to their roost.

"So these pigeons will leave to find their own food, and they'll always return to this room to roost. So . . . if you think it's okay to eat pigeons, then you have a con-

stant food source that doesn't need to be fed. And you
never have to exit the building!" She had to admit it was
very clever.

She looked up at the rows and rows of nooks. But
there were so many birds! Hundreds and hundreds.
Whoever had designed this room had created a supply
of food that allowed one to *never* leave the Institute.

Josephine shuddered and sat down in her new
prison. This room was loud and it stank and she felt
quite miserable. Fargus was supposed to show her how
to get home tomorrow, and now she had ruined it by
getting caught. She could kick herself for being so stupid. Hadn't Ida told her to stay in the cellar?

She didn't think it would be possible to sleep. But as
the meat pies digested, her eyes became heavy and her
anxiety and fear finally took their toll. She fell asleep sitting up, surrounded by feathers.

EIGHT

The alarm bell woke Fargus. He hoped it had nothing to do with Josephine. He wanted to go check on her in the cellar, but he dared not go without Ida, and she was in the girls' room down the hall. So he could only lie there, the loud clanging of the bell rattling his skull.

Most of the time, Fargus didn't mind living in the Institute. Not really. It meant he got to spend time with Ida. He always felt safe with her. And for some reason, she always knew what he wanted to say, even when he couldn't say it. He had liked visiting Josephine, too, but the desire to communicate with her had been too overwhelming. He had returned to the shed to fetch Ida and bring her back with him to act as his voice, but then Josephine showed up at the Institute.

It had all been so frustrating. He could convey to

Ida some of the things he had seen at Josephine's house using the secret, silent language they had developed over the years, with hands and facial expressions, but he'd been unable to share all the vivid details of his visit. He could tell that Ida hadn't really believed he'd gone anywhere. But now Josephine was here and Ida knew he was telling the truth, so it was all okay. Except . . . now they were all stuck here and not in Josephine's big clean house that was full of lovely food.

Fargus tried not to think much about his life before the Institute, although he still had the occasional dream. Usually in the dream, he and his parents, Margaret and Jasper Dudson, were in a giant lighthouse, which was where Fargus had been born. He saw his mother laughing and chasing him up the stairs, up and up and up, and when he reached the top, there was a blinding light and his father would grab him and shield his eyes. Fargus would erupt into a fit of giggles, and it was here the dream would end.

In Fargus's memory, playing games with his parents had always been interrupted. Meals had rarely been finished. One of them, his mother or his father, had always been running up to stoke the beacon. The light had been to guide the sailors out at sea into a safe harbor so they wouldn't hit rocky shores. His parents had kept a huge box of coal outside and had been forever fearful of running out, because the coal fueled the fire that created the big light.

When Fargus turned five, it became his job to get the coal. "Ship coming! Run and fetch the coal, Fargus!" was what he heard all day long. But he found collecting coal terribly dull. He just wanted to go to school like normal children.

One day Fargus was playing outside and he began to follow a trail of ants. Fargus was fascinated by ants and the way they could carry food that was twice as big as their teeny frames. He liked to picture himself carrying an enormous banana twice as big as his own body. This day, he really wanted to see where the ants were headed. So he followed them from the edge of the lighthouse across the lawn and into the nearby trees. Fargus was always supposed to be within hearing distance of home, but he was having such a marvelous time that he completely disregarded his parents' rule about leaving the lawn. Lost in his harmless diversion, he didn't hear his father shout down from the lighthouse, "Ship coming! Run and fetch the coal, Fargus!"

But Fargus was in the trees.

His father yelled down again. "Hurry, Fargus!"

This time, Fargus lifted his head, thinking that *perhaps* he had heard something.

"Fargus, hurry! The ship is coming!" his father pleaded.

This time Fargus was sure. His father was calling for coal. He leaped up and ran out of the trees, across the lawn to the coal box. He shoved lumps into a bucket as quickly as he could and ran back to the house as fast as his feet would take him. He ran inside and up the stairs—up and up and up. He reached the top, where his father grabbed the bucket and shoved him backward.

"What's wrong with you, boy?!"

Fargus's heart sank. His father had never raised his voice at him before.

His father fed the fire, which had died to a sad sputter. The fire started to spark and grow but Fargus's father didn't stop. He kept shoveling in panic. From outside along the coast Fargus heard an earth-shattering collision, as if a giant had stepped on an enormous egg. The lighthouse rumbled and swayed and he was thrown to the floor.

When he stood back up, his father was weeping. Fargus had never seen a man cry before, and he was frightened. He knew that his mother always made him feel better when he cried, so he ran downstairs to find her, but she wasn't in the house.

She was standing out on the cliffs, staring down at the ocean. Fargus ran to her and was about to ask her to go upstairs when he saw what she was looking at. A large ship—six sails at least—was smashed against the rocks. A fire blazed and men were jumping into the water, swimming for the safety of the shore, only to be pulled under by the current. Fargus heard screaming, smelled smoke, and felt the explosion of gunpowder.

"Can we help them?" Fargus asked.

"No," his mother said in a grave voice. "They are finished. As are we." She turned and walked back to the lighthouse.

That night, as Fargus lay in bed, he heard his parents fighting downstairs. He heard his name uttered several times, and he awaited his punishment. The fight didn't end, though, until early in the morning. His mother entered his room, eyes red from crying, carrying a small sack. As she knelt by him, she explained in a soft voice that he needed to leave the house immediately. At first Fargus thought this was his punishment, but she told him that they were all in danger. The Master's servants would be arriving soon to interrogate them about the shipwreck. She made him get dressed and handed him the sack of bread and meat. Fargus wished she would yell at him or spank him. Nothing was worse, he thought, than her sad smile.

He walked numbly downstairs to the front door. His father instructed him to hide behind the coal box until the interrogation was over. His parents walked him outside, and his father said that if anything should happen to him and his mother, Fargus should follow the rising sun. His father shook his hand, as Fargus had seen him do with adults, and his mother bent over him and whispered into his ear, "We love you." Then she tucked a family picture into his pocket.

Fargus crouched behind the coal box as he was told, afraid that his trembling was audible. Soon he heard the sound of men on horseback approaching the lighthouse. Although he could see nothing, he guessed there were around a dozen of them, and before Fargus's parents could say a word, the men dismounted their horses and accused Fargus's father of negligence. He was responsible, they said, for repaying a debt to the Master equal to the price of a vessel, a hundred men, livestock, and rare spices found only on the Isle of Sharlen. When his father said he didn't have the money, the men seized both him and Fargus's mother. Fargus could hear her crying as they tied her up and forced her onto one of the horses. His father, a tall, robust man, did not struggle, and Fargus knew it was because he was afraid of the men discovering his son.

All the while Fargus listened, wanting to cry out, wanting to help. But when he opened his mouth, ready to protest, to scream, he found, to his horror and surprise, that nothing came out. His voice had abandoned him.

He sat for one week, waiting for his parents to return, neither eating nor drinking, refusing to budge. But after ten days with no sign of them, he began walking east- ward, as they had ordered him, and this was how he had found the Institute. Stairway Ruth, delighted at his arrival, had let him in and Kitchen Maggie had fed him. They questioned him about his past, but he just stared straight ahead, never wanting to talk again. After a few days, they stopped trying.

The alarm downstairs ceased ringing, and Fargus was jolted back to the present. He thought of Ida and Josephine and wondered what they would think of him if they knew what he had done. Would they be as ashamed of him as he was of himself? Sometimes it was better not to speak.

NINE

Josephine had been asleep just a few hours when the pigeons began squawking. She woke with a start and looked around, confused. Where was she?

A fragment of light was streaming through the square window above her. Josephine stood up, stretched her aching body, and looked outside. The sun had risen and for the first time she could see outside. With a sinking heart, she knew that she was a very, very long way from home.

The landscape before her was a wild plain, with short grass and little other vegetation. And it went on for miles, with no other signs of life in sight. No people, no buildings or houses. No wonder Ida had said Josephine should stay inside the Institute. There was no other place to go.

What could have happened to her in that shed? How

could she have traveled so far, so quickly? Perhaps, like in many of her storybooks, there was magic out there that she had never heard of. And Josephine found that, despite her fear of this strange, new place, she was a bit thrilled with the idea that the world was not as straight-forward as she had been led to believe.

She continued to gaze at this new land. There were trees outside, but only a handful. The trunks were white and the leaves were bruise purple. The tops of the trees were completely flat, as if they'd been chopped off with a scythe. They were beautiful, and Josephine was so mesmerized by them that she wanted to run down and climb one immediately. But her enthusiasm was soon quelled.

She was looking at one of the trees when out of the corner of her eye she saw something dart across the plain—a dark blur, moving at high speed, running on all fours, like a huge dog or bear. And then there was a second blur, running toward the first.

As the two figures collided, they fell upon each other ferociously, rolling around and kicking up dust. It seemed like a normal battle between beasts until one of them stood up like a man on its hind legs and began to walk toward the other. Then the other one stood up. Josephine saw now they were much too big for dogs. They were almost the size of the trees.

They circled each other, flexing their enormous back muscles and stomping their clawed feet. They had thick coats of what looked like black fur running from their foreheads down their backs and into their tails. But as the sun hit the creatures, she saw that it wasn't fur at all. It was more like spikes or quills. These animals were covered in thorns, like the cacti she'd studied in school.

She gasped, and the two creatures, though hundreds of yards away, seemed to hear her. They turned simultaneously toward her window. She ducked instinctively, but even as she took cover, she knew she was being ridiculous. It was impossible that they'd heard her.

She rose and looked out the window again. To her horror, the two creatures were back on all fours and they were running straight toward her!

Josephine's heart pounded. She felt frozen. She could now make out their faces, and they were like nothing she'd ever seen before. Pointed ears stuck up out of square heads. Each creature had beady yellow eyes and a muzzle that ended in a piglike nose.

But most horrifying and terrible of all was . . . these animals had *no mouths*.

Instead, they had taut brown skin that reached from the bottom of their noses down into their necks, where even more spikes rose. The lack of lips or teeth or any opening at all made these creatures look wicked beyond any monsters Josephine had ever conjured in her imagination. She was frightened down to her soul.

What could these terrifying animals be? Was she safe up in the tower? Could they climb a vertical stone wall? Surely not. But what if they could fly? Josephine ran to the door, but it was bolted shut. She pounded on it as hard as she could.

"Help! Help me! Please!" she cried. The creatures would be at the base of the tower any second. She yelled again, "Help me!" But she knew even as she said it that no one would come. Why should Kitchen Maggie or Stairway Ruth care if she was in despair? She decided to try a different tactic. Maybe they had no concern for her, but they most certainly cared about their meat supply.

"Fire!" she screamed. "Help, quickly! There's a fire!"

Sure enough, she heard heavy footsteps approaching the doorway. The bolt slid back and Kitchen Maggie thundered inside, holding a large bucket of water. The pigeons squealed in alarm.

"Where is it? Where's the fire?" she spat.

Josephine hadn't really figured out what she would do if anyone came. She shrank into a corner and pointed at the window. "There are monsters out there! And they're coming to get me!"

Maggie clamored to the window and looked. After a moment, she turned and glared at Josephine. "You've summoned the Brothers. I should throw you out the tower and let them have you."

She stomped across the room and grabbed a pigeon from the nearest cubbyhole. She broke its neck in one swift motion. Then she grabbed another and another, killing each of them with the same ease and pleasure. She took them to the window. A wild snorting was coming from below, and she tossed down the dead birds one at a time.

"Give these to the Master. Go home! We'll have merchandise ready for him in two days!" The snorting stopped.

Josephine stared at the door Maggie had left open behind her and began creeping toward it.

She was about two feet away from the doorway when she felt herself being hoisted up by the back of her shirt. Maggie spun Josephine around so that they were face-to-face.

"If you do anything to attract the Brothers, or start screaming again, or do anything that I find even slightly irritating, I'm going to take my mallet and pound you into meat stew. Got it?"

Josephine hung there, helpless and petrified, feet dangling. "Yes, I've got it."

"Good." Maggie dropped her and stormed out of the room, bolting the door once more.

Josephine cried out when she hit the floor. "Ow!" But she figured the pain was better than what the Brothers might have had in store for her. She pictured their mouthless faces and huge claws and decided that if the Brothers were always prowling around outside the Institute, she would stay inside and learn to love the taste of pigeon.

TEN

Josephine rested against the wall and stared at the pigeons, wondering if they were as bored as she was. They had nothing to do, just like her, and yet their twitchy heads and unblinking eyes gave them a sense of alertness, which was the opposite of how Josephine felt. She was exhausted, and every so often her eyelids would close, her head would droop, and she would fall into a sort of half sleep.

But then a pigeon would fly in through the window and cause pandemonium all over again. Each time one returned, the birds squawked as if it hadn't ever happened before. The arriving bird usually had something in its beak, and it would fly to its little cubby and share whatever it had found with the babies and other pigeons that were anxiously awaiting lunch.

Josephine was amazed by them. All of the pigeons

had the option of flying out of this prison forever and making a lovely new home out in the wild, and yet they chose to return each day to this disgusting tower and take care of their families. Perhaps that was what the noise was about when they returned. Maybe it was a celebration.

Josephine wondered, if she and her father were pigeons, would her father return to feed her? Or would he make a break for freedom—

Her ruminations were interrupted by voices on the other side of the door. "Stop holding on to my trousers or I'll pop you in the mouth!"

Josephine suppressed a giggle. It was Ida! She didn't think she'd *ever* been so happy to hear someone's voice. She heard the bolt on the door slide backward, the door creaked open, and Ida's head and then Fargus's came peeking around. Josephine grinned at them. "You found me!"

Ida sashayed into the room, smirking. She was wearing the same cotton clothes as two days before, and Josephine suspected she had even slept in them. "I knew exactly where they'd put you." Fargus looked at Ida incredulously, so she added, "Well, maybe we looked a *few* other places first."

Fargus, looking the same as he had that day in her garden—rumpled and vaguely embarrassed—walked up to Josephine and handed her a sweaty lump of cheese and a piece of bread. Josephine gratefully shoved both into her mouth. The three of them sat in a tight ring in the cleanest corner of the room.

"Uhhh faw dothers," she told them.

"Can you finish chewing and say that again?" Ida asked.

Josephine swallowed. "I saw the Brothers." She wiped her mouth and moved some of the curls from in front of her face.

Ida's eyes widened. "The Brothers? They were here?"

"Yesterday. And they were running right toward me."

"They saw you?" Ida was gobsmacked.

"I cried for help, and then I cried fire, and then Kitchen Maggie came up here and threw out some pigeons, and then they went away."

"They went away? Did she say anything to them?"

"Uh . . . yeah . . . she told them that she'd have 'merchandise ready' for the Master 'in two days.' Who is the Master?" she pleaded.

Ida's face fell and she cursed quietly. "Hot maggot breath, I thought we had a few more weeks."

Fargus suddenly looked frightened.

"What?" Josephine asked. "What's the matter? What kind of merchandise is she talking about?"

"*Us*," Ida groaned. "Fargus and me. *We're* the merchandise."

"What do you mean?"

"Every month Maggie and Ruth give an orphan to the Master."

No one had yet told her who the Master was, but Josephine could tell from the fear in Ida's voice that he must be very horrible. "So how do you know it will be you or Fargus this time?"

"Because we're the only two left."

Josephine felt sick. "What do you mean? There aren't any other children here?"

Fargus shook his head.

Josephine tried to process this information. She had a terrible thought. "Maybe Kitchen Maggie meant me. Maybe *I'm* the new merchandise."

"I wish," Ida said thoughtlessly, "but Stairway Ruth can't wait to get rid of me. Ever since I put that mouse in her bed . . ." She stood up. "This changes everything. Fargus, is our bag ready?"

He stood up too and nodded his head confidently.

"Right," Ida said. "We don't have much time. We have to leave while it's still dark."

"Leave? But . . . but . . ." Josephine stammered. "You mean, take me back to my house, right? Because we'll be safe there. There are no Brothers or Master or—"

"Kitchen Maggie has locked the cellar so we can't get back in. And even if we could, we might not be able to find the passage in time. Fargus told me it took him hours and hours to find the exact right spot. We can't risk it. We have to leave tonight."

Josephine felt tears forming.

Ida added, "Plus, it will really help us to have a third person, right, Fargus?"

Fargus nodded.

Josephine didn't care. She didn't want to be the third person. She didn't care if she saw Ida or Fargus ever again. She just wanted to be home.

"No. I won't do it. I won't go."

"Fine. You can do whatever you like," Ida replied with a dismissive wave of her hand, "but Fargus and I are going, and then the only one left to give to the Master . . . is *you*."

Josephine began to panic and felt desperate to talk them into staying. "But what *happens* if you get taken to the Master?"

Ida's green eyes flashed with anger. "Kids get taken to the Master and they never come back. Ever. Do you understand?" She got in Josephine's face and growled, "The Master murders children, peels off their skins, and then eats their *bones*. Maybe you want to meet him, but I would rather take my chances outside."

Josephine trembled. "But the Brothers—"

Ida cut her off. "Only come out during the day, which

is why," she added in a casual tone, "we have to leave tonight. Are you coming or not? We don't have time to argue." And with that she marched out the door and down the stairs.

Fargus took Josephine's hand like a caring friend and pulled her toward the door. Josephine couldn't believe it. She actually wanted to stay in the smelly pigeon room. At least then she would still be in the Institute, close to the strange passageway that had brought her here. If she left, perhaps she was giving up her only chance of ever getting home.

However, the logical side of Josephine knew that Fargus and Ida had been in the Institute far longer than she and that they probably knew what they were talking about. And she had no one else to trust. So she begrudgingly let Fargus pull her to the door, and the two of them followed Ida down the stairs.

Before Ida opened the door at the bottom of the stairs, she turned to them and said, "Stairway Ruth will be checking the classrooms now. We have less than ten minutes to grab food and the bag." Josephine and Fargus nodded, and Ida opened the narrow door with a creak. The coast was clear.

The three of them did a quick raid of the kitchen and grabbed dried meat, cheese, and bread. After they had all they could carry, they tiptoed into the dining hall, careful to avoid the loose floorboards, and Josephine saw enough tables and stools for a small army. A large grandfather clock stood in one corner. Fargus walked up to it and opened a wood panel that revealed the inner mechanics of the clock. Josephine noticed a canvas sack had been shoved into the clockworks.

Fargus removed the sack and shut the panel. He tiptoed back to the girls, and Ida took the sack and placed their foraged food inside. Josephine could see that there was already a decent stash of food in the bag. Ida and Fargus had been planning this escape for some time.

"Now for the hard part," Ida said. "We have to steal the key to the front door off Stairway Ruth. It should be easier, now that there are three of us." She smiled at Josephine, who smiled uneasily back, knowing that she had been given very little choice in the matter.

Ida whispered her plan to them twice, to make sure that everyone knew what he or she had to do.

ELEVEN

Stairway Ruth was in a grand mood. She marched happily through her evening patrol, twirling her lashing stick. This new child was an incredible stroke of good luck. She and Maggie had been worried for some time about what they would do once they ran out of orphans. They had no idea if the Master would allow the Institute to survive if they had no children to give him.

And tomorrow they were handing over Ida. The beauty of it! Ida was the most troublesome little brat Ruth had ever known and she was happy to get rid of her. Fargus was tolerable because he made no noise. But he had become Ida's little lackey, which Ruth detested.

And now fortune had smiled upon them, and this other strange girl had appeared, which would buy them another two months at least to find more children. Ruth felt she had been given a wonderful reprieve.

She strolled through the doorway into the library and her foot caught on something. Before she knew it, she was flying face-first into the floor. As soon as she landed, she heard a voice cry out, "Get her!" It was Ida, that little demon! Ruth lifted her head and reached out for her lashing stick, but instead she saw Fargus crouching there, already holding it.

"Don't mess with me, children!" she screeched. "I'll boil your eyeballs!" Ida suddenly leaped out of nowhere, landing on Ruth's back and pinning her down. Ruth reached with her sinewy arms and tried to grab her.

And then something dreadful occurred.

It was something out of Stairway Ruth's worst nightmares.

The child began *to tickle her.*

It started directly below the ribs. Ruth summoned all of her courage and strength and vowed not to give in. But it was no use. A great guffaw escaped from her lips, followed by a cackle, and then, worst of all, a giggle. She was completely incapacitated. And, at the same time, furious. There was nothing she hated more than laughter, and her own was the most detestable of all.

"Hurry!" Ida yelled. "Get the keys. Now!"

Josephine emerged from her hiding place, bent down next to Ruth, and began to search for the keys.

"In her right side pocket! Quickly!"

"I'll . . . get . . . you . . . Ida . . ." Ruth panted between fits of laughter.

Josephine's fingers were shaking, but she finally managed to get her hand inside the pocket and extract a large ring of keys. "Got 'em!" she cried.

"Put. Those. Down," a voice commanded from behind her. Josephine turned and saw Kitchen Maggie, looking like an angry bull about to charge. Josephine did the first thing that came to mind and dove into Maggie's blubbery middle. Maggie was thrown off balance and seemed to fall backward in slow motion.

She landed on her ample backside with a booming thud, crying out as Josephine's tumbling frame knocked the wind out of her.

Josephine lay there, shocked and sprawled on top of the mammoth woman.

"Josephine, quit lying around! Let's go!" Ida cried, grabbing their food sack and scampering toward the front hall. "Come on!"

Josephine struggled to extricate herself from Kitchen Maggie, but it was like trying to climb out of an over-size marshmallow. She felt she'd never reach the edge. Finally she managed to pull herself up onto her feet and start running. Fargus ran beside Josephine, but without warning he stopped, turned around, and returned to the two defeated women. Both Kitchen Maggie and Stairway Ruth were struggling to catch their breath and stand up.

Josephine cried out, "Come on, Fargus! What are you doing?"

Fargus held Ruth's lashing stick, and a crazy look came over him. He approached Ruth from behind, took careful aim and hit her once, hard across the rump. "Aaaaarrr," she screeched, in pain and fury.

He then leaped toward Maggie, still supine on the floor. Her eyes were bulging in alarm as she simpered, "Now, now, Fargus. I always treated you well. Remember that day I let you have extra porridge?"

Fargus raised the stick once again, whipped it through the air, and let it land on the bottom of Maggie's bare feet. "Aaaaghh," she screamed.

Fargus gleefully ran to catch up with Josephine and Ida, and the three of them sprinted through the hallway.

Arriving at the foyer, Josephine stared at the towering set of doors before her. She guessed they were three times as tall as she was. They had been built to keep children inside and, more important, to keep the Brothers out.

Ida placed an iron key in one of the massive doors

and turned it with both hands. Josephine heard three loud clicks and the door groaned open a crack. Ida grinned with satisfaction but then the alarm began to ring. *CLANG! CLANG! CLANG!*

They heard a mechanical groan and looked up to see a latticed gate lined with metal spikes begin dropping from the ceiling, about to separate Josephine and Fargus from the open door.

"Hurry! NOW!" Ida ordered, and was halfway out the door when Josephine was overcome with doubt. Perhaps if she left this place, she'd never make it home, never see her father or her books again?

"Wait!" she cried.

Ida froze. "What?"

"Are you *sure* this is the only option?" Josephine looked at Fargus and could see that he was feeling uncertain as well.

Ida pointed at the descending gate. "It's a little late to change your mind, don't you think?"

They could hear Maggie and Ruth yelling from the library. "Ida! Fargus!"

Ida gritted her teeth. "Either come with me and have a *chance* of survival, or go to the Master and have none. Which is it going to be?"

Josephine knew that once they were through this door, there was no turning back.

"We have to go, *now!*" Ida commanded. "Come on!"
She disappeared out the door.

Josephine knew she had no choice. She looked at
Fargus, who seemed to be hypnotized by the falling gate,
which was already at eye level, and grabbed his sleeve.
She pulled him under the gate and shoved him through
the crack in the doorway. But he hit her in protest. She
whirled around to find out what was wrong and saw
that he had dropped the sack full of food. The gate was
almost closed when Ida stuck her head back inside and
hollered, "Hurry up!"

Josephine thrust Fargus toward Ida, and with all the
courage she could muster, she dove for the sack. She
knew that any second the gate could crush her like an
ant. She grasped the bag and crawled back under the
gate, the metal spikes just grazing her calves. She had
made it out just in time.

She ran outside into the cold night air, turning back
to see Kitchen Maggie and Stairway Ruth stuck behind
the closed gate, reaching for her, screeching like ban-
shees, "You'll never survive out there!"

Ida giddily shut the door in their faces.

There was sudden silence.

Fargus stood in the darkness, shocked that Josephine
had risked her life to go back for their food. She handed
him the recovered sack, and he embraced it as if it were

his lost child. Ida looked at Josephine with a newfound respect and said, "You nearly got pinned like a bug!" Josephine guessed by the tone of her voice that this was a compliment.

Ida looked back at the Institute one last time. "Good-bye, Kitchen Maggie. Good-bye, Stairway Ruth," she whispered. "May you each choke to death on a pigeon bone." And with that she started running, expecting Fargus and Josephine to follow.

Fargus scuttled after her, but Josephine couldn't get her feet to move right away. Her heart pounded as she surveyed the dark plains spread out in front of her. This was it. She took a deep breath and hurried after the others.

TWELVE

It was a cold night with a small moon. Josephine wasn't sure she had ever known such blackness. She looked up, hoping to take comfort in the stars, but saw none. A blanket of clouds had left the sky a matte gray.

They had been walking for more than an hour. After the sprint from the Institute, Ida had decided they could slow down for a bit, so Josephine reasoned that Ida must not believe they were in immediate danger.

She trusted Ida knew where she was going, but mostly she just hoped that Ida was right about the Brothers coming out only during the daytime.

The one noise she heard was the squelching of her own galoshes—*squish, squish, squish, squish*. Josephine found herself mesmerized by the rhythm of her steps: one, two, three, four, one, two, three, four.

Suddenly Ida stopped walking and swung around. "Shh. No talking."

"But I wasn't!" Josephine whispered back.

"You've been babbling for five minutes!" Ida insisted.

Josephine looked at Fargus for support but he nodded, apparently in agreement with Ida. She had indeed been talking to herself. Josephine was happy the darkness covered her flushed face. "What . . . what was I saying?"

"Some nonsense about a factory shaped like a duck," Ida answered. "And can't you walk any quieter?"

"Sorry," Josephine offered. But her boots were too big. There was no way to suddenly make them the right size. Ida scowled and kept walking, and Josephine concentrated on keeping her heels in the backs of the boots, which seemed to make them less floppy.

The land seemed to go on and on. Josephine couldn't see much in the dark, but she had the feeling she was walking on an endless savanna. The grass was short and dry, and the beautiful purple trees had disappeared. *What other animals might be lurking in the dark?* she wondered. *We're safe from the Brothers, but what about wolves or snakes?* She wanted to ask Ida but was afraid she'd snap at her again, so she kept quiet.

Josephine was exhausted. She imagined them all walking on and on until they died from old age.

●●●

Fargus followed Josephine closely. He didn't like the dark, but he hated being alone even more. As long as he was with Ida and Josephine, he felt a sense of calm. He looked at Ruth's lashing stick in his hand and felt it was a sword that could protect them from whatever might come out of the shadows. He gripped it tightly and tried to concentrate on something besides the darkness, like the food he would be eating when they finally stopped for a rest.

Ida's head was buzzing. She and Fargus had been planning their escape for months, and she could hardly believe it had worked. But their escape was just the beginning of their trials. Only Ida knew where they were headed, and only she understood the kind of dangers they would face.

She knew it was important not to show any fear. Fargus and Josephine looked to her for leadership. So she tried to think about something else, something soothing that would distract her from the challenges that lay ahead.

When Ida was little, she had hated bedtime. So each night when her parents had tucked her in, they would tell her a story to help her relax. The tale was always the same: the story of how her parents had met. Ida now imagined her mother and father walking beside her, telling it to her once more in their calm, loving voices.

"The Dorringtons have always been hunters," her father would begin. "And when I was young, it was my duty to go into the countryside and gather meat for the citizens of Gulm. The problem was, I *hated* hunting. I tended to prefer animals to most people. But I did greatly enjoy the outdoors, so most days I would find a field of wildflowers and lie on my back and waste away the hours just daydreaming. Once in a while, I would fire my gun into the air so that people within earshot would assume I was working. And then, when it was nearly twilight, I'd shoot some rodents and take them back to town. I had all the inhabitants of Gulm believing that the larger animals had migrated away and that I was a gifted hunter to even find rats for them to enjoy. And they ate them up—yum, yum!"

Ida always laughed at this part, and her father would take the opportunity to tickle her. It was only when Ida got a little older that she realized he must have been teasing her about making people eat rats.

"It was a beautiful autumn day," he'd continue, "and I'd just turned eighteen. I was lounging by a brook, drowsy and lazy, and I lifted my rifle and fired it off into the distance—*bang*. But then I heard someone squeal—*eek!*—and fall. My heart froze and I ran as fast as I could toward the sound.

And I found a girl, a little younger than I was, lying on the ground with her leg bleeding. She was unconscious and I didn't know what to do. I nearly fainted.

"To examine the wound, I needed to lift her skirt a bit and remove her stocking. I'd never touched a girl before, and I was terrified. Once I could see the wound, I saw that it was superficial. The bullet had only grazed her leg. I had never been so relieved in my life. I gently lifted her and carried her to the brook—"

"Just say *Mommy*!" Ida would interrupt.

"Okay, sweetie. I carried Mommy to the brook so I could wash the wound, but as soon as her foot touched the water, she woke up and cried out—*aaoohh!*"

Ida would giggle and say, "And you almost dropped her, right, Daddy?"

"That's right. I was so surprised, I almost dropped her. I set her down on the shore and said"—at this point, her father would adopt an exaggerated stammer—"'I . . . um . . . I was trying to . . . uh . . . wash your leg.'

"I wet my handkerchief and handed it to your mother. She wiped away the dirt and blood, and I was able to really look at her for the first time. She was slight and had brown hair in need of a wash, and spotty skin."

Ida's mother would playfully slap Jon on the arm. He would ignore her and keep talking. "But she had the reddest lips I'd ever seen, and they were so full that I guessed she must bite them all day long. Finally she spoke and said, 'I can't believe how corn-brained that was.' And I was so ashamed, Ida. I told her, 'You're right. I'm a fool. You should have me *arrested!*'

"But your mother replied, 'Not you! Me! I know you fire into the air every day. I've seen you do it, and yet I climbed a tree so I'd have a better view.' Oh, Ida, I was afraid the whole town knew of my lies, so I got defensive. 'How do you know I fire into the air? And have a better view of *what*?'"

He would then bat his eyes and in a high-pitched voice do an impersonation of Ida's mother. "'Of you . . . I come here every day to watch you.'" Ida would giggle.

Then back to his angry voice: "'To watch *me*?! Are you a spy?! Who sent you?! What have you told them?'" He would take his wife's hand in his and smile. "That's when the most terrible thing happened. The girl, your mommy, started to cry. I was in complete despair. I'd never even spoken to a girl before and here I'd shot one and made her cry in the space of an hour. If this was courtship, then it was much harder than I'd ever imagined. I knelt beside her and pleaded, 'I'm sorry I yelled. I just don't understand why you were watching me.'

"And she confessed that she watched me *every* day, on her way to collect pinecones. '*Why?*' I asked."

At this point, Ida's mother would always chime in. "It never occurred to him that he might be attractive."

"I had a beaky nose *and* I was too tall *and* my hair would never lay flat," to which Ida would say, "Your nose is *still* beaky!" and her father would tickle her again.

"I wanted her to go see Doc Shuster, in town, so he could check her wound, but she didn't want her mother to know what'd happened. She said she had to get home and change clothes before she got in trouble." Jon would grab his heart in mock pain and say, "So she left me! Arrrgh!"

"Stop exaggerating, Jon," her mother would say, rolling her eyes.

"She *did* ask if she could come back the next day."

"He blushed like a ripe strawberry!" her mother might add.

"As soon as she was gone, I couldn't wait to see her again. And lucky for me, she came back the next day. . . ."

"And the next . . . ," her mother added.

"And the next . . . ," Ida chimed in. "And the next . . . and the next . . . and the next!"

"It took you a week to even ask my name!" her mother taunted.

"'Elizabeth,' she told me, but I preferred to call her 'Bet.' We were married two months later."

"And then you had *me*!" Ida cheered.

"Yes, then we had you," her father cooed.

"And when you grow up one day," her mother would always add, "*you* might be lucky enough to be shot by someone you love."

This was the signal that it was time to say good night. Her parents would tuck her blanket in tightly, and kiss her on the forehead, and she would always sleep soundly, knowing they were just in the next room.

Those days had been pure bliss for Ida. She and her parents had lived just outside of Gulm, and Ida had spent her days running and playing in the woods.

Everything was heaven until the Master, the merciless ruler of Gulm, decided to prepare for a new war. The Master attacked a neighboring mining town, reasoning that he might, perhaps, someday need more metal, so that he could, perhaps, someday make more weapons, should he, perhaps, maybe, just in case, ever have to go to war.

Jon and Bet Dorrington opposed the idea of war, and so when soldiers arrived at their front door and told Jon to hunt extra food for the growing army, he refused.

He was shot on the spot.

Ida had been observing from the kitchen, and she was confused and thought that the soldier must have been in love with her father, because that was the only reason she knew to shoot someone. But Bet ran out from the bedroom, grabbed Jon's gun, and told Ida to run. Ida didn't want to leave, but the insistence in her mother's voice made her do as she was told. She climbed out the window, jumped, and rolled onto the grass below. Ida heard a second shot and turned in time to see her mother fall to the ground next to her father.

Ida's screams of horror drew the attention of the soldiers. They started toward her. Ida ran into the woods and didn't stop running or crying for three days. By the end of day three, she could weep no more, and she decided she had used up her life's supply of tears.

By this time, she was far from the woods that she knew so well. Ida was in a land she had never known before, with short grass and purple trees. She soon came upon the Institute, the only structure in a sea of nothingness. She was dehydrated and on the verge of starvation when she knocked on the door and was yanked inside.

That was five years ago. Ida hadn't been outside since. Until now.

Ida's feet were numb from walking so long. She and Fargus had been walking around barefoot for years, having no one to buy them new shoes. Around the Institute that had been fine, but last night, when she had first got outside, she had felt every rock and twig. She hadn't complained—she was not one to show weakness. Now that her feet were too cold and numb to feel anything, Ida was relieved, knowing that this was for the best. She would be able to travel as far as necessary.

THIRTEEN

The night sky became a dull blue as the sun fought to appear on the horizon. Josephine noticed that the landscape had changed yet again, and the shapes that had seemed so ominous during the night were actually clusters of boulders littering the plains. Seeing the rocks now, she understood how she could've mistaken them for sleeping monsters.

"You thought they were sleeping what?" Ida asked.

Josephine blushed. She was thinking out loud again. "Nothing."

This time Ida was kind enough to let it go.

As the sun began to peek out at them and illuminate the landscape, Ida stopped walking. She looked at them both and announced, "The Brothers will be waking soon."

Josephine looked around in terror. "What do we do?"

"We hide," Ida answered matter-of-factly. She started toward a mound of boulders where an overhanging rock formed a cavern seemingly big enough for the three of them. They stretched out side by side, and Fargus was asleep the moment he laid his head down. Ida and Josephine lay staring at the cavern ceiling and nibbling on small bits of food.

"Ida, why does everyone call them the Brothers? Are they related?"

"Who knows? Maybe it's just because they fight like brothers. Stairway Ruth liked to tell us stories before we went to bed, just to scare us. She claims that one time there was this girl, Laura, who dropped her favorite doll out an Institute window, and she climbed down using her sheets tied together to fetch it." Ida's voice got dark and menacing. "That night, when Stairway Ruth finally discovered the sheets hanging out the window, she pulled them back in and all that was left was a severed hand clutching the fabric."

Josephine felt she might be sick. She put down her bread and cheese.

Ida took no notice and kept munching on a piece of pigeon jerky. "But I don't really believe that story. I mean, who drops their favorite doll out a window?"

"So they ate Laura?"

"Exactly."

"But . . . how could they? They don't have any mouths."

Ida wrinkled her brow; this had never crossed her mind. "Maybe they just tore her apart with their big claws?"

Josephine shuddered, but her curiosity compelled her to ask, "Where do they come from?"

"Kitchen Maggie had a lot of theories. But Stairway Ruth said they're creatures from the Dark World and that their kind was used as hunting dogs for King Brokhun, who rules the underground kingdom. And the Brothers were just cubs, still suckling at their mother, when an evil witch found her way to the Dark World and stole them away. They were so sad at being taken away that they became full of vengeance and spite. Now they work for the Master because he promised to take them home to their mother one day."

Josephine felt chills climb her back when Ida mentioned the Dark World. "Are we really safe from them right now?"

"The fact that we're sitting here talking to each other is a pretty good sign that we're safe . . . for the moment."

"Is there any way to fight them?"

"Well, I think it's safe to say that a doll won't do any good."

"Why do you always make jokes about such serious things?!" Josephine snapped.

Ida looked as though she'd been slapped and said coldly, "I have no idea how to fight them. We just have to hope they don't see us." And with that she closed her eyes and turned her back to Josephine.

Josephine scolded herself for snapping at her friend. She had so many more questions to ask! Where were they headed? Who was the Master? Were there only two Brothers, or was there a whole pack, waiting to attack them? She settled against the cold, hard rock and promised herself that she would ask Ida these questions the moment she woke up.

FOURTEEN

Fargus was the first one to wake. He had dreamed he was a pigeon. He was too fat to fit back through the window of the pigeon room, so he had flown all night over the dark plains and purple trees, knowing that soon he would become too tired to flap his wings and would fall into the claws of the Brothers. The dream had left him more exhausted than he'd been before he had slept. He stood up and stretched. Josephine was sleeping soundly with Ida curled into a tight ball against her. Fargus needed to pee.

He walked around the boulder, out of sight of the girls, and while he relieved his bladder, he imagined the cheese and meat waiting for him in their sack. He couldn't remember the last time he'd been so hungry. He started to walk back to the cavern when he smelled something sour, like rotten pork growing hot among dead leaves.

He looked around and froze in his tracks. Not twenty yards away, lying underneath a tree, was one of the Brothers. Up close, the creature looked twice as huge and terrible. Fargus waited to see if he had been spotted, but the Brother didn't move, so Fargus slowly looked over his shoulder, because where there was one Brother, there was always another. He saw nothing but grass and rocks.

On cat feet, he made his way back to the crevice and shook Ida awake. Just as she opened her mouth to admonish him, he covered her lips with his hand. She could see from the look in his eyes that they were in trouble. She grabbed Josephine's wrist and squeezed.

Josephine awoke with a start and sat up immediately, as if she had been dreaming of this moment all day. Using his hands, Fargus tried to explain what he'd seen. Ida quickly put the food into the sack and signaled for them to follow her outside, away from the Brother. But as Josephine went to put her boots on, Ida shook her head no.

Josephine knew she was right. The noise would give them away. So she nodded and carried the boots in her arms.

They rapidly made their way down the side of the boulders and onto the ground. Josephine had never felt a stronger urge to run, but she knew that for the moment, silence was more important than speed. She felt horribly vulnerable in her bare feet.

Ida motioned for Fargus to keep an eye on the one Brother while she scanned for the other. Ida felt that if they could just make it to the next set of boulders, they would be safe. Her eyes played tricks on her as she searched the horizon. Every shadow and rock became the other Brother.

Their progress was excruciatingly slow, and Josephine felt as if she were walking through glue. Fargus was close behind her, never taking his eyes from the beast under the tree. He was concentrating so deeply that he didn't watch where he was going and ran right into Josephine, who squeaked in surprise.

They all glanced at the tree. The Brother lifted its head, scratched its ear, readjusted its massive frame, and settled back down. Josephine breathed a sigh of relief and looked at Fargus, who nodded his apology.

Ida had been watching the scene impatiently when, all of a sudden, she sneezed.

Josephine and Fargus whipped around and looked at her in horror. Then Ida sneezed violently two more times—*Achoo! Achoo!* None of them had to check to see if the Brother had heard as a furious snort filled the air. Josephine felt hot fear boil in her stomach, push up into her throat, and suddenly come out of her mouth in a high-pitched scream. "RUUNNNN!!"

All three of them bolted across the plain in separate directions. Ida had planned to lead them to the next set of boulders, but she hadn't had a chance to explain her idea. So now she raced for the rocks, while Fargus headed back to the cavern they had just left. And Josephine, all on her own, hurtled into the great wide-open plain.

Josephine ran without direction as fast as her feet would carry her. She sprinted over rocks and coarse grass, her soft feet feeling every sharp edge and harsh blade, but deep down she knew that she could never outrun a Brother.

She dared to look over her shoulder and saw that the hideous creature was not chasing her, but was circling the boulder where they had been sleeping. She slowed down and looked for Ida and Fargus, but to her dismay, she could see only Ida.

The Brother stood on its hind legs and stuck its wet snout into the crevices of the boulder, trying to locate the boy it knew was inside. Fargus pressed himself against the inner wall of the crevice, knowing he didn't have long before he would be clawed to pieces.

Josephine tried to figure out a way to help him when she heard an ominous snort off to her left. That's when she saw it.

The other Brother was heading straight for her.

She screamed and took off running again. Her lungs burned and felt as if they might burst, but she willed her legs to be stronger and faster than they'd ever been before. Every second, she anticipated the force of the Brother's weight on her body, the claws on her flesh. She thought, *My father will never know what happened to me*, and then, with sorrow, *Maybe he won't even care.*

She heard a terrible growl just over her shoulder as the Brother leaped. She tensed and waited to be crushed. But he landed in front of her. She skidded to a stop, nearly impaling herself on the huge thorny body. The Brother reached down with one spiky paw and gave her a light flick, throwing her several feet onto her back.

It was playing with her, like a cat playing with a tiny mouse.

She landed with a thud, but her adrenaline was pumping so hard that she didn't feel a thing. She popped back up, never taking her eyes off the monster. It glared at her, its yellow eyes narrowed in concentration. A disgusting green liquid oozed from its enormous snout. Josephine thought of Fargus's lashing stick and cursed herself for not bringing a weapon of her own. She had nothing but her father's stupid boots. Out of frustration, she took one of the boots in her hand and hurled it at the Brother.

The heel hit it squarely in the eye. With a loud grunt, it reeled back in surprise.

Josephine threw the second boot, careful to aim this one, and managed to hit the other eye this time. The Brother wailed in pain like a bear trying to scream through its nose: *Heeeawww!* His eyes were closed and leaking some horrible yellow fluid.

Josephine knew this was her only chance. She ran back in the direction she had come from, and as she looked up, she saw Ida standing on a group of boulders, waving madly. Josephine sprinted toward her.

At the sound of the second Brother's anguish, the first Brother jerked up from the boulder where Fargus was hiding and ran toward the tortured cry. Fargus crawled out of his hiding place and spotted Josephine running toward Ida. He, too, took the opportunity to escape and ran toward where Ida was waving.

Ida reached down and helped both of them up the rocks, saying, "Nice shot, Josephine!"

"But my boots—"

"If you hadn't got rid of them, *I* would've. I've found a fantastic cave that's too small for them to enter. We should be safe there. And Fargus"—she raised an eyebrow at him—"this time, no wandering off!"

Fargus looked sheepish. He nodded in agreement.

Josephine wasn't about to let Ida off that easily. "And no sneezing, *anyone*."

Fargus smirked, and for the first time since Josephine had known her, Ida looked contrite. "Right," she said. "No sneezing."

Ida led them to the new cave, and for the next several hours the three of them slept as hard as the rocks surrounding them.

FIFTEEN

Ned Mosley strolled up Main Street while his father, Morgan Mosley, limped behind. Ned was grouchy today because his feet hurt. His shoes were too small. This seemed to happen every few months now. Ever since he had turned fourteen last year, Ned was growing faster than an overfertilized cornstalk, but he hated to complain about the tightness of his shoes, knowing his father couldn't afford to buy another pair. He was determined to endure the pain for a few more weeks at least.

The sun had yet to rise and most of Gulm was still fast asleep. This was Ned's favorite part of the day. Two brooms were cinched to Ned's back, and tied to his belt was the cloth sack full of biscuits and ham his father had prepared the night before.

Ned had been going to work with his father since

he was old enough to hold a broom. Morgan's leg had been irreparably damaged many years ago, and the job of town sweeper had become too much for him on his own. So Ned had begun helping with the work, despite his father's protests. Ned preferred work to school any day. Still, his father insisted on lessons at home so that Ned wouldn't be "an ignorant dullard."

Today was warm and blooming trees had left a thin layer of pollen over the streets and sidewalks, so Morgan and Ned got right to work. It would take them all day to finish. Ned untied the brooms, handed one to his father, and began to clean one cobblestone at a time. Ned could hear his father humming an old song about sailors' wives.

Thirty sparkling cobblestones later, Ned heard someone approaching. He looked up to see Angus the bellman walking toward them with displeasure. Ned saw his father put his head down and keep sweeping, hoping Angus might go away. Angus had been working in the bell tower for more than fifty years, and the constant ringing seemed to have shattered his manners.

Angus placed his angry, ruddy face directly in front of Morgan. When he spoke, big flecks of spit landed on Morgan's lapel.

"Someone's comin'!" Angus sprayed.

"How are you, Angus?" Morgan gently replied.

"Dog brains on moldy toast. Someone's comin'!"

"Who's coming, Angus?" Ned knew his father wanted them to get back to their sweeping. They still had 894 cobblestones left to clean.

"I saw 'em from the tower! I was about to sound the mornin' get-yer-bums-out-of-bed-and-get-on-wit-yer-bloody-useless-lives alarm when I seen 'em! Comin' out of the forest!"

Morgan sighed. "Who, Angus?" Angus was renowned for being an unreliable source; he spent most evenings licking the walls of the local pub.

"Children! Three of 'em!"

Suddenly Morgan was paying attention. "Children? Are you sure?"

Angus squinted at Morgan as if he were the small print on an unsavory invoice.

"Aye, I'd bet me life on it. Three wee figures, headin' this way. Lookin' knackered and hungry—"

"Which way?" Morgan interrupted.

"Down toward the ol' bridge. 'Bout a mile away. Shall I sound the alarm?"

"No. I'll take care of it."

"That's right kind of ya, mate. I much appreciate it. I hate to have to fill out a report. I always get ink on me face." Angus began backing away toward his tower. "Ya know what they say, sir. Being a bellman always takes its toll. Get it?" He looked at Ned. "Do ya get it, lad?"

Ned rolled his eyes.

"And make sure ya tell me when yer birthdays are—I'll make sure to give the bell an extra tug for ya!" He turned and skulked back to the tower.

Morgan immediately turned to his son and said, "Ned, you must warn the children not to enter Gulm. Run along the riverbed and the fields so no one spots you. Go, quickly!"

Ned dropped his broom and did as he had been instructed, no questions asked. He weaved in and out of the streets and reached the bottom of the hill in no time. He crossed a long field that belonged to Alma and Bruce Jarvis and was almost to the riverbed when he heard voices. He dove into the long grass and looked toward the main path he had taken great care to avoid.

There, walking toward the Jarvises' home, were Alma, Bruce, and three children. There were two girls and a younger boy. The girls seemed only a year or so younger than Ned. One was tall with crazy hair, and the other was shorter, with black hair and angry eyes. The boy hung back from the rest of the group, but the girl with big hair was chatting happily to Alma and Bruce as if they had known one another their whole lives. Sadness flooded Ned. He had failed his task. He was too late. The strangers were done for.

SIXTEEN

Josephine couldn't remember ever having been so happy to see an adult. She, Ida, and Fargus had been walking for days, and they had run out of food that morning. Ida had managed to navigate them out of the plains, but there hadn't been one berry or drop of water to be found. Josephine's feet were blistered, her legs ached, and her tongue felt as if it were made of wool.

It was dusk when Ida found the well. They were walking through a pasture when Ida squealed as if bitten. Josephine spun around, afraid the Brothers had found them, but Ida broke into a giddy run and stopped at a small round wall that Josephine soon realized marked the top of a well. Ida was so happy that she almost dove into the water. The three of them were on their third bucket of water when Alma Jarvis came upon them.

It was odd. At first Josephine had been sure Alma meant them harm. She was a chunky woman in her fifties and she had rushed toward them with menace in her eyes. But when she reached Ida, she opened her arms for a warm embrace. "Hello, children! Hello there!" she called out, laughing. She welcomed all of them with a hug, as if they were lost family. Josephine must have only imagined the flash of anger she thought she had seen. And now they were all walking back to Alma's house with her husband, Bruce, who was as tall and thin as Alma was short and round. He was older than Alma and walked as if he suffered from arthritis. He told the children they could call him "Spruce Bruce," his nickname from childhood, and then he invited the three of them to bathe and have dinner. When Alma heard their stomachs growl, she chortled and suggested dinner first.

They soon arrived at the Jarvises' house, which reminded Josephine of a chocolate cake. It was dark brown with swirly white trim along the roof. And when she walked inside, she felt instantly cozy. Every surface seemed to be covered with a bright crocheted blanket, and Alma had a colorful collection of teapots that sat on the hearth above a well-used fireplace. Bruce immediately lit up the fire as Alma disappeared into the kitchen to brew tea and start supper.

The children plopped into worn chairs with plump ottomans, and they were so exhausted from walking that they all fell asleep immediately, waking up only when an irresistible smell seeped in from the kitchen.

Dinner was a sumptuous feast of duck and roasted parsnips. Alma was a wonderful cook. There was warm bread, fresh churned butter, and spinach from the garden. Afterward, Bruce lit his pipe as the five of them gathered in the living room. Alma served the children hot chocolate and caramel cakes, while she and Bruce drank tea.

Josephine didn't know food could produce such contentment. Her belly was full, her eyelids heavy. She was just about to nod off to sleep again when Alma asked in a casual tone, "Where do you children come from, then?"

Half-asleep already, Josephine heard herself say, "Not from here. I fell through the shed." Her eyes flipped open. She hadn't meant to say it. It was as if her mouth were completely disconnected from her brain.

"A shed? Whatever do you mean, dear?" Alma asked.

Despite the fact that her brain knew that her story made her sound out-of-her-head crazy, she told them more. "Fargus came to see me at my father's house, and I tried to find him, but instead I fell through a wall and woke up at the Institute."

Alma's face scrunched in confusion.

Josephine looked at Ida and Fargus for support, but both were sound asleep.

"Start from the beginning, hon. Don't rush. Perhaps Bruce and I can help you." Alma stared at her, her intense eyes willing Josephine to tell her *everything*.

And Josephine did. She felt a deep desire to tell these people anything they wanted. She told them about Fargus's appearance in her garden, her tumble through the shed, the Institute, Stairway Ruth and Kitchen Maggie, and the encounter with the Brothers, and she also told them about her father, his gloves, and his total lack of interest in her.

"And who is your father, dear?" Alma asked.

"Mr. Russing," she answered.

Bruce and Alma exchanged a look. It reminded her of the look people gave at home whenever his name was mentioned. But how would they know him here?

She could have talked all night; she was so relieved to tell someone about her predicament. These were adults, nice, responsible people who would help her get home. She was in the middle of the story about her schoolteacher and the silly, squashy tomatoes when she drifted off to sleep, with the hot chocolate mug still delicately perched on her lap.

SEVENTEEN

Ida awoke in a strange bed, covered in layers of old blankets. She looked over and saw Fargus similarly buried in the bed next to hers. For all she knew, they might have been sleeping for days. She labored to remove the heavy blankets, noting that a smaller child could have been stuck under their weight indefinitely. She got out of the bed, stretched, and looked around.

The room was completely bare. They were in some type of attic and she had no idea what time of day it was. Her keen sense of curiosity got the better of her and she decided to have a look around the house. She opened the attic door and walked down the narrow stairs until she reached the landing. Voices were coming from downstairs. Ida had learned to be an excellent eavesdropper at the Institute and she crept toward the voices with catlike silence.

It seemed to be some sort of meeting. There were many people present and they all kept trying to talk at once. Ida knew immediately that they were talking about her, Josephine, and Fargus.

A strange voice said, "I say send them back to where they came from."

"But what if the Master hears of it?" This sounded like Alma.

"Better to just turn them in now," another strange voice said, and was followed by a murmur of agreement.

"But what about the one that claims to be a Russing?"

"She could be of real value."

"A bargaining chip."

"But how will you keep her here?"

"Will you use force?"

"No, no. She's weak-minded. We'll keep her here with kindness," Alma answered her inquisitors.

"Very well. So we all agree?"

"Yes, we agree."

"Then it's settled. All three of them shall be kept here until we decide otherwise."

"Fine. Thank you, Mayor. We feel much better."

"You're welcome. And thanks for the tea, Alma. You always have the lightest cakes in Gulm."

Alma tittered with pleasure. Ida heard the front door

open, and several men walked out. The moment the door closed, Bruce announced to Alma, "If that man gets any fatter, his constituents will have to carry him around in a wheelbarrow."

"Bruce! What if he hears you?"

"He's gone, Alma."

"I swear that man's shadow has ears. Go wake the children. I'll get breakfast ready."

Ida crept from the landing and scurried back to bed, where she found Fargus wide awake, looking at her fearfully, unable to move underneath the layers of down. She pretended she was asleep and signaled for Fargus to do the same. By the time Bruce opened the door, they were both pictures of innocence.

EIGHTEEN

Josephine awoke feeling completely refreshed. Sunlight streamed through the window above her bed. She looked around and saw she was in the room of a young girl. She gasped at how near it came to the bedroom she had fantasized living in when she was younger.

There were dolls piled in a corner, smiling blankly up at the new day. A small rocking horse held a teddy bear, and tiny sprouts of lilac decorated the walls. Fresh tulips had been left by Josephine's bedside and she could see they were just about to open. Brightly colored books sat on a blue bookshelf and a piggy bank rested on top. There was a beautiful dollhouse in the corner, a perfect replica of the Jarvises' house, swirly white trim and all.

Josephine stepped out of bed and looked out the window. It was a gorgeous day and she could see Bruce heading out to the fields. She turned to explore the room some more, and when she opened a door, she discovered a large pink bathroom.

She ran a scaldingly hot bath—just as she liked them—and happily lowered herself into the deep tub. She began scrubbing away what felt like a month's worth of dirt and grime. Once her skin was clean, she tilted back her head and submerged her thick nest of curls.

Underwater, she began to hear all the noises in the house as they reverberated through the porcelain and bathwater. Footsteps downstairs, a door shutting above her, the *drip-drip* of the faucet. She instinctively stuck her big toe into the tap to block the leak, just like at home. *Home.* She sighed, realizing to her surprise that she was starting to miss it less and less.

There was suddenly a voice at the door. "Josephine, dear, are you in there?"

Josephine sat up, water running into her eyes. "Yes, Alma."

"Come on out. I have something for you."

Josephine spotted a fuzzy towel hanging on the back of the door. She climbed out of the bath, dried off, and wrapped herself in the towel.

She opened the bathroom door to find Alma standing there, beaming, holding a cornflower blue dress with matching shoes. "I thought these looked like your size."

A dress! Josephine had never owned anything but pants. And this dress had long bell sleeves and a nipped-in waist, like the older girls at school wore. She grinned happily. She jumped back into the bathroom and slipped on the dress. It fit fairly well, though it was a little long in the sleeves. But the color—oh, the color! Josephine thought it was the most beautiful blue she had ever seen. The shoes were big, but not nearly as bad as her rubber boots had been.

She stepped out to show Alma, who clucked her tongue in approval, but then: "There's still one problem."

Josephine looked down at the dress, wondering if the long sleeves looked silly.

"Your hair, dear. It's a disaster."

Josephine's hand went up to her wet mop of tangles, and she flushed with embarrassment.

Alma sat on the bed and patted the spot next to her. Josephine went over obediently and sat down. Alma held a large wooden brush and she began to painstakingly work on Josephine's matted hair. It was painful, but Josephine didn't want to appear ungrateful, so she didn't wince.

"Alma?"

"Yes, dear?"

"It's daytime, and I saw Bruce outside."

"Yes?"

"Isn't he afraid the Brothers will get him?"

"No, dear. The Brothers don't bother us inside the borders of Gulm."

"Why not?"

Alma yanked at a particularly nasty knot, pulling Josephine's head backward. "We made . . . an agreement with the Master many years ago."

"What kind of agreement?"

"Nothing a young girl like you should worry about," she said curtly, signaling that the conversation was over.

It took an hour for Alma to unknot the nest of tangles Josephine had accumulated. But when she had finished, she was quite pleased with herself. She turned Josephine to face her. "That's more like it." She then reached into her apron and pulled out a headband, the same blue as the dress. "And it would be nice to see that pretty face for once." She used the headband to gather up the hair that usually fell in Josephine's eyes.

She tilted up Josephine's chin, examining her handiwork. "You're a real beauty, hon. You should stop hiding it." Josephine shone with pride. No one had ever called her beautiful.

Alma stood to leave. "I'm going downstairs to make you some hot chocolate."

Josephine stood too. "Thank you . . . for everything."

Alma shooed her with her hand, as if to say, "It's nothing," and then left the room.

A large oval mirror stood in the corner and Josephine went over to look at herself. She didn't recognize the girl that stared back at her. She hadn't been gone from home for very long, but she already seemed more mature. The dress covered her long, gangly limbs and gave her a look of ease. Her hair shone from Alma's brushstrokes, and with it out of her face, her eyes were bigger and brighter than ever before. Josephine felt far away from the awkward, shy girl she'd been at home.

Suddenly, Ida came bursting through the door. "Get your stuff! We have to get outta—" Ida froze when she saw the new Josephine. Her jaw dropped. "What happened to you?"

Josephine's heart sank, and Ida could see the effect of her words on Josephine's face. "I mean . . . uh . . . you look pretty." Josephine half smiled, not sure if Ida was lying.

"Thank you."

"I'm glad you're dressed. We gotta get out of here."

"Why? What's wrong?"

"I heard them talking about us. They want to keep us here for the Master."

"What? Alma and Bruce don't work for the Master."

"Yes, they do!"

"They can't! They're the nicest people I've ever met!"

"But it's not *real* nice—it's *fake* nice. I'd rather someone just spit in my face than be fake nice."

Josephine shuddered at the idea that Alma was just pretending to be kind. She felt tears form at the idea of being on the run again. "I don't care what you say. I don't want to leave." She crossed the room and picked up her dirty shirt and pants. She removed her gloves from her pants pocket and shoved them into the pocket of her new dress. She would need them when she finally got back home.

"Listen to me," Ida said. "They had a meeting. The whole town is in on it—even the mayor!"

Josephine crossed her arms. She would not be persuaded. "Alma and Bruce said they would help me find a way home, and I trust them."

"Fine," Ida said. "Then Fargus and I will leave without you."

Josephine studied Ida's face, wondering if she was bluffing. "Fine."

Ida didn't blink. "Fine."

NINETEEN

She's gone crazy. It's the only explanation."
Ida stood, arms crossed, in the front yard of
the Jarvises' house. Fargus sat spinning on a
wooden swing. "Or maybe they hypnotized her. Either
way, you and I are outta here!"

Fargus didn't appear to be listening. "Fargus! You
and I are leaving, right?" Fargus stopped spinning and
looked at Ida, indecision in his eyes. "I don't believe it!
You too? This was never part of our plan! We were supposed to refill our provisions in Gulm and then scram.
You're my best friend, Fargus, and I'm telling you, these
people are creeps!"

Fargus stared hard at Ida. Then his gaze crossed the
yard and landed on Josephine, wearing her new blue
dress, picking yellow flowers in the neighboring field.
Ida spit on the ground in disgust. "I know you don't

want to leave her, but we *have* to! This place is a trap.
Josephine has gone nutty as peanut pie. It's just you
and me now. And I am not sticking around Gulm!" But
Fargus shook his head firmly no.

Ida growled and stormed off down the road. She
turned her head every thirty feet to see if he was following.
Finally she stopped and kicked a fence, muttering, "Why.
Won't. Anyone. Listen. To. Me?!" She broke through a
piece of wood in the fence and then she stomped around
and kicked up dust for a while. Winded and sweating,
she walked back to Fargus and said in as calm a voice as
she could muster, "Fine. You can have one day. One! But
then we're leaving. With or without her." Fargus smiled
and went back to his spinning.

Josephine had had a wonderful day. She'd collected
daisies all morning, swam in the stream in the afternoon, fished with Bruce, and then napped on a warm
rock until dusk. Alma greeted her at home with more
hot chocolate. Josephine had never known such good-
natured people and she knew in her heart that Ida was
wrong about them. She knew it as certainly as her name
was Josephine. These people would never harm her.

That evening, as she returned to her pink and laven-
der room, she was once again touched by the sweet baby
dolls in the corner, with their tiny lace dresses and red

heart lips. She fell asleep dreaming of bubbling streams and thrashing fish, never stopping to wonder about the child who had once inhabited this precious room and where she was now.

Alma and Bruce stayed up late into the night, whispering about their guests and preparing more of the hot chocolate. Alma thought it was all going very well, but Bruce was suspicious of Ida. He noticed that she rarely smiled and seemed to always position herself near the door. He would be relieved if she made an escape. It made him uncomfortable to have children around.

Their own daughter, Sarah, had been with them for nine precious years—which was longer than most, but had felt as short as a hug good-bye. He and Alma never talked about her, but he could often see in Alma's eyes that she was thinking about her. Some families in the town kept having children so that they might never know a silent dinner table, but he and Alma had been unable to have any more. Sometimes he fantasized about going after Sarah, but in his heart of hearts, he knew he was a coward. If he failed to find Sarah, he could lose Alma and his house, and he didn't think he could bear to lose anyone else.

Alma finished stirring the chocolate and went to find a jar.

"What if she doesn't want any more chocolate?" Bruce asked.

"Then we'll drug her milk. Don't worry—that girl's happier than a cow in a pasture. She's not going anywhere."

Bruce nodded in sad agreement. He held the jar and covered his nose and mouth as Alma poured the warm liquid.

TWENTY

Josephine could barely keep her eyes open. If given the chance, she could have slept all day. It seemed the longer she spent here with the Jarvises, the more tired she became. But the journey to get here had been very exhausting. Perhaps she just needed to catch up on some rest. She felt her eyelids begin to flutter closed again when the door to the bedroom opened.

Alma entered carrying a tray that held porridge and a mug of hot chocolate. Josephine couldn't believe it, but she was almost starting to get tired of chocolate.

Alma placed the tray on the nightstand next to Josephine's bed and took a seat in the rocking chair in the corner. "Good morning, dear. How did you sleep?"

"Fine, thank you." Josephine sat up, willing herself to feel more awake.

"I'm glad to hear it. Because I have news."

Josephine began to eat her porridge, feeling too tired to care much about what Alma had to say.

Alma smoothed her apron. "Ida and Fargus are gone."

Josephine stopped chewing. "Gone? What do you mean, 'gone'?"

"They ran away in the middle of the night. When I went to wake them this morning, their beds were empty, and meat and bread had been taken from the kitchen."

"But how . . . how could they leave me without saying good-bye?" Josephine felt the tears start to run, grief cutting through her drowsiness.

"I don't know, dear. That girl, Ida—well, it's obvious that no one's bothered to teach her any manners at all."

"But they were my friends." Suddenly the porridge was thick and dry and sticking in her throat. She didn't want to believe it. Her first real friends and they had abandoned her! Maybe they hadn't really been her friends at all.

"Did they tell you they wanted to leave?" Alma prodded.

Josephine wiped at the tears on her face. "They left because Ida didn't trust you. She said that you and Bruce were working for the Master."

Alma tittered. "Me and Bruce? Oh, no. Never, dear. We would never harm children. Why don't you drink your hot chocolate? It will make you feel better."

"Ida wouldn't listen to me."

"You don't worry your head about it. Those two will run out of food and they'll come back in no time."

"Really?"

"Yes, really. I've already got Bruce out there searching the woods for them."

Josephine began to breathe a little easier. "Thank you, Alma." She was now less worried about Ida and Fargus, but no less hurt that they had chosen to leave her behind.

"You finish your breakfast and your chocolate and then come on downstairs. Today I'm going to teach you how to sew."

Josephine nodded and did as she was told.

TWENTY-ONE

Fargus groggily awoke out of a hard sleep to find himself surrounded by a circle of strange, gawking children. He jumped up, shocked that he was no longer with Ida in the attic of the Jarvis house. He was now lying in a round room made of silver metal, which created reflections everywhere he looked. Instead of the dozen children standing around him, there appeared to be hundreds of them, and none of them was Ida! He saw his own confused face mirrored on the floor and walls and ceiling.

He instinctively reached for Stairway Ruth's lashing stick, which had been tucked into the back of his pants. But it was gone.

The children continued to gape. He had never been the focus of so much attention and curiosity. He didn't like it.

"He's awake," one of the girls whispered.

"Go on, ask him," said another.

A boy stepped forward. "What's your name and where are you from?"

Fargus opened his mouth, knowing it was futile. He did his best to say his name but nothing emerged—only a kind of sigh.

"Are you from Gulm?" the boy asked.

Fargus shook his head.

"Did you bring us any news?"

Fargus shook his head again.

One girl began to get impatient. "Can't you talk?!"

Fargus looked at her, defiance building in his belly, and shook his head again.

The children seemed to collectively deflate with disappointment and they drifted away, no longer interested in this newcomer.

Fargus was glad to be ignored as he assessed his new environment. The round room had no apparent door and the walls curved into the ceiling. The absence of doors or windows made Fargus feel claustrophobic.

He stood up and circled the room. As he neared other children, they would move away. He felt diseased, completely unwelcome. He was desperate to know where he was, but he could not catch anyone's eye long enough to ask.

Finally he stopped circling the room, sat down, and

stared at the others. Fargus observed them for well over an hour, and he concluded only one thing.

These children frightened him.

They weren't like other children. They didn't skip or jump or shove one another. They didn't make up things or sing for no reason. They weren't silly. They sat or stood in groups and talked in low whispers.

It reminded him of when he'd been young and his parents had taken him to a neighbor's house for dinner. The adults had sat and talked and talked, and Fargus couldn't wait to get away and return to his real life of throwing things. He felt that way now, out of place and bored. He wished he could tell Ida about it.

Where was she? Did she know he was here? And what about Josephine? He hoped they were both nearby. He wanted to leave this place as soon as possible.

Suddenly everyone was in motion, scurrying this way and that as if they'd been given a signal, but Fargus hadn't heard a thing. The children grew more and more agitated and all whispering stopped. A mounting energy permeated the room and Fargus could sense that something was about to happen. All the children migrated to one side of the room, leaving Fargus by himself. He felt sick to his stomach. The silence tasted like cold chalk.

Then he could hear faint footsteps outside. They grew closer and closer, but came at an unbearably slow rate.

Fargus's heart thumped in his chest, each beat a warning cry: *run, run, run.* A large door, invisible to Fargus
the moment before, slowly opened on the far side of the
room. The other children closed in on themselves like a
sea anemone. Fargus was even more exposed and alone.

An old man with a crooked back and a little orange
hat entered the room. He was nothing like the dragon
that Fargus had been expecting, and the boy exhaled.
In fact, the old man looked a little foolish, which in
turn made him look kind. The man approached Fargus,
took off his hat, and introduced himself. "Good afternoon. My name is Mr. Seaworthy. I have come to invite
you to lunch with your host. Do you accept?"

At the mention of lunch Fargus's stomach lurched.
He hadn't eaten since yesterday. He looked back at the
children. They were so close together that their breathing seemed to intermingle into one lung gasping for air.
He knew they were afraid, but he couldn't imagine it
was because of this old man. He wanted to ask them
what he should do. But he was just as afraid of these
pale, trembling children as he was of Mr. Seaworthy. He
nodded his acceptance at the man, who smiled pleasantly and replaced his little orange hat. "Wonderful.
Won't you come this way?"

Fargus followed him out the door, which promptly
slammed shut behind him.

TWENTY-TWO

Josephine sat in a shady spot in the overgrown field behind the Jarvises' house, practicing her sewing but without much success. After she made a stitch in her cloth and pulled it tightly, as Alma had taught her, the thread would come out of the needle, and Josephine would have to hold the needle up to the light and try to get the fraying thread back through the tiny eye. It took countless annoying jabs to finally get it through again.

As she went to make the next stitch, she would remind herself not to pull too hard this time. But as soon as she stabbed the cloth with the needle and began weaving it through, she would forget and do it again. Her teeth ached with concentration.

Recently it seemed her mind had turned to mush. Trying to wrap her head around hard facts was like trying to read a newspaper that had been rained on. For

Josephine, who had always relied on her sharp mind, this was the worst kind of frustration.

She sighed, looked up, and screamed when she spotted an older boy standing not two yards away from her in the field! He was staring at her as if she were some kind of rare bird. He was tall with a wide forehead and freckles, and he wore a brown cap that sat on his head at a slight angle. He moved toward her and spoke gently. "I didn't mean to scare you."

"Alma!" she cried. "Bruce!" They had warned her against talking to anyone from the town, even children.

"No! Please be quiet! I'm here to help you. My father sent me to make sure you and the others were all right."

Josephine froze. "What others?"

The boy was confused. "The friends you arrived here with, the girl and the boy."

Josephine looked as though she might laugh. "Friends? But I don't have any . . . friends . . . do I? No. I'm certain I don't." She dropped her sewing and her face crinkled as if she had been accused of forgetting her homework.

The boy was now looking at her as if she were a helpless toddler. "What's your name?" he asked.

"My name is . . . um . . . it's . . ." She looked up at the sky, hoping the clouds might spell it out for her, but nothing came.

"My name is Ned. I'm the sweeper's son." Ned had

never met anyone who couldn't remember her own name. He smiled and took a step closer to her. "What have you got there?"

She was befuddled and he motioned toward her fabric and thread. She shrugged at the cloth as if it belonged to someone else.

Ned looked deep into her eyes, which were an extraordinary amber, but they looked a bit dull, as if they had been dipped in wax. She smiled at him blankly, having already forgotten the conversation they were having. Ned began to wonder if the Jarvises had done something to this girl.

He decided there wasn't a moment to lose. He crossed over to Josephine, picked her up, and slung her across his back like one of his brooms. Josephine squealed protests and yelled for Alma as Ned scuttled away from the Jarvises' farm as quickly as possible.

Josephine beat her little fists across his back, but it was no use. He was stronger than she was. Ned walked on for twenty minutes before he found what he was looking for—the Cherry Spring. No matter what time of year it was, this spring was always sure to be mind-numbingly cold. Or, as Ned hoped in this case, mind-*awakeningly* cold. He approached the edge of the water, swung Josephine back and forth three times, and then threw her into the icy spring.

She screamed and thrashed as if she were being attacked by wasps, and it suddenly occurred to Ned that maybe she couldn't swim! Panicked, he was about to dive in after her when she swam to the edge and rushed out of the freezing water. He tried to wrap his jacket around her but she responded by shoving him to the ground.

"Are you crazy?! You kidnap me, you try to drown me, and you pretend to know me and my friends!" At the mention of friends, her face filled with horror. "Fargus and Ida! Where are they?" She looked around her, teeth chattering with cold and shock.

"You've been staying with Bruce and Alma Jarvis, on a farm. Do you remember?"

Her eyes looked wild. "Uh . . . yes . . . I think so . . . yes."

"Your friends were there with you. I saw them. Do you remember them being there?"

Josephine had a hazy memory, more like a dream, of Bruce showing Ida and Fargus how to bait a fish line. "I . . . I think so."

"Concentrate. Are they still on the farm?"

Alma making lunch. Bruce building a fire. Sleeping. Ida angry at her. Why? Alma in her room. Chocolate. Crying. Sleeping. "Alma said they ran away." It was all coming back now, snippets of memory.

"Alma was lying. And I think she's been drugging you."

"Drugging me? Why would she do that?"

"She's working for someone else. The whole town is."

Josephine knew he was talking about the Master. She tried to keep the tears from forming, not wanting to accept the truth, that she had been betrayed by Alma and Bruce, her new family.

Josephine began to back away from Ned. "Why should I trust *you*?"

"I could've left you on that farm, unable to say your own name."

She tried to read his face, which was kind and gentle, but so was Alma's. She had no idea *whom* to trust anymore.

Ned saw pure panic in her eyes. "Can you tell me your name now?"

"Josephine Isabelle Russing."

Ned looked as if he'd been punched in the gut. "Russing? Who else here knows your name?"

"Just Alma and Bruce."

"I need to get you to my father. Now."

"I'm not going anywhere with you." Josephine pulled off her soaking headband and attempted to harness her wet hair, which was already starting to refrizz. She managed a semidecent ponytail and then turned her attention to her clinging, now dirty new dress and her mud-caked, ruined blue shoes. "Hot maggot breath," she muttered, and then blushed when she realized she had used one of Ida's curses.

Ned glared at her, annoyed with the delay. Why were girls so maddening?

"Fine. Stay. I'm going home to a warm fire. Just be careful of the Brothers." He walked toward the forest.

Josephine stopped preening and looked into the trees, suddenly nervous. "Do they come around here?"

Ned didn't even turn around. "I guess you'll find out." He marched into the dense forest, leaving Josephine shivering in the open clearing. She turned in circles, trying to get her bearings. It was difficult to see the sun, so she didn't know which way was west. She heard a rustling in a nearby bush and decided not to wait to see what it was.

She ran into the forest after Ned.

TWENTY-THREE

Ida awoke in complete darkness. She smelled damp earth and there was something uncomfortable sticking into her back, but when she turned to remove it, she found she couldn't move. Her hands and feet were bound. She struggled and pulled at the ropes, but they had been expertly tied. The more she fought, the tighter they grew, and the more panicked she became.

She yelled into the darkness, "Fargus! Fargus, are you here? Can you hear me? Josephine?"

Her voice traveled upward and then echoed back down. Bits of dirt fell from above and landed in her eyes and mouth. She spat them out and decided she was in a cave or hole of some sort and that the thing poking at her back was probably a root. She tried not to think of the bugs and worms that could be sharing her prison.

Tears soon formed and Ida told herself that it was just the grit in her eyes, but deep down the terror was growing as she accepted her fate.

She was completely alone in the dark.

TWENTY-FOUR

Fargus was led down a long corridor made entirely of marble. The ceiling, the walls, and the floor were the same polished shade of opalescent white, which made Fargus feel as if he were inside an enormous pearl. The old man in the orange cap moved slowly. He appeared to be in some pain. He was bent over at such an extreme angle that Fargus reckoned the man could smell his own shoes.

Finally they arrived at a large door set deeply into the wall. It, too, was made of marble, but it was black and covered in large carved replicas of the Brothers, their malicious eyes daring anyone to enter. To Fargus, the door suddenly felt as ominous as the Brothers themselves.

Mr. Seaworthy tapped on the door ever so lightly and it slid backward with a *whoosh*.

"*Bon appétit,*" he mumbled, putting his hand on Fargus's back and nudging him inside.

Fargus entered an enormous room, more appropriate for a ball than a lunch. He could see a dining room table on the far side of the space and approached it tentatively. As he got closer, he could see the table was large enough to seat fifty men, and each chair looked as though it had been carved from a whole tree. But they were all empty. There was no one at the table. Had this been some sort of trick?

And then a reedy, nasally voice called out to him, "Have a seat."

It came from the head of the table. Fargus saw that someone was sitting there after all. It was a child, no older than ten, he guessed. The child had a large, round head and dark, squinty eyes, and his black hair only served to accentuate his pale, spotty skin. He wore black from head to toe and had several chunky rings on his tiny hands. The behemoth chair surrounding him gave the impression of a toddler resting in an upright canoe. As Fargus stood there gawking, the boy began to squirm. He attempted a smile but it came out as more of a sneer. Fargus decided that this must be some sort of boy prince and that his parents would be joining them soon.

"You are hungry. Sit down." The dark boy gestured toward the far end of the table, his voice bored and patronizing. Fargus trudged to the other end and climbed into his chair/canoe. As soon as his bottom had touched the seat, a bell rang and several large men entered with food and drink.

There was stuffed goose and ham and pheasant. There were potatoes in various fashions—mashed, roasted, and au gratin. There were peas and beans and long cobs of sweet corn. The men poured wine for the prince and tea for Fargus, and then they added desserts to the table—pomegranate pudding and dark chocolate treacle surprise.

Fargus stared at the feast in front of him. Each one of these dishes was a favorite of his, but he didn't trust the food. Something in this room was dangerous, and Fargus didn't know what it was yet. Fear rose to his throat and left only bile. He knew if he took even one bite of food, he would ralph all over the table.

He looked at the silver pitcher of water sitting in the middle of the long table. One of the servants saw his wistful gaze and immediately fetched it for him. He poured a glass for Fargus, who gulped down every last drop. The glass was refilled immediately and Fargus drank it. This was repeated four times. Finally Fargus felt he was full and he sat back and crossed his arms in satisfaction.

The boy in black stared at him, bemused. He, too,

had not eaten any of the feast. Instead he had watched Fargus enjoy his water. He smiled his same snarky grin and began to laugh. "I have been inviting children to dine here for years and this is the first time any of them has chosen to gorge himself on water. What is your name?" Fargus stared at him silently. "No matter, I know it already. I was just being polite. It's Fargus." Fargus's eyes bulged in surprise. "Oh yes, I know everything, really. Care to test me?" Fargus looked down at his empty water glass.

The boy continued, barely missing a beat. "You are a person of few words. I like that. Everyone else comes in here and just yammers away at me while they choke themselves on my food. It is very unpleasant. You would hate it. But why waste words and time? Let's move on to more interesting topics. I have one I think you will enjoy very much. It's called 'The story of the careless family who lived in a lighthouse.' The beginning is a little boring, but I think you'll find the end very engaging." Fargus looked straight into the boy's cold, black eyes and realized with horror that he was sitting with the only person in the world who knew his parents' fate.

This pale boy dressed in black was the Master.

TWENTY-FIVE

Josephine caught up with Ned and he led her smugly out of the forest and into Gulm. Ned gave her his cap and told her to keep her head down and not draw any attention to herself. Everyone around them was busy with their own tasks. Men polished windows outside of shops, rearranged merchandise, and triple-checked cash registers. Women set up vegetable stands, and bakers kneaded dough behind flour-dusted windows.

Ned smiled and waved at several people who knew him. Josephine felt their eyes upon her, so, as instructed, she looked down at the cobblestone streets, careful to hide her face. She was relieved no one had confronted them, and just as she was about to breathe easier, someone called out to Ned, a plump woman with a face as red as exposed brick.

"Ned, oh, Neddy! I have sweet potatoes for your pa, sweet pea." She came out from behind her vegetable stand with considerable effort and walked toward them with a paper bag in hand. "I've been saving them for him special. I know they're his favorite."

Josephine cast a nervous glance at Ned, who had plastered on a big fake smile. "Thanks, Beatrice." He took the paper bag and started walking on, but Beatrice hit him playfully on the shoulder, almost knocking him into a fruit stand. "So when is your pa going to let me come over and cook those up for him properly?"

Ned regained his balance and peeked quickly at Josephine. Beatrice caught the look and noticed Josephine for the first time. Her eyes widened when she realized that she had never seen this girl before. Strangers were a rarity in Gulm, especially children.

"Neddy? Who is—?"

"We really have to be going, Beatrice. Thanks for the potatoes." He tried to walk away, but Beatrice grabbed him and said, a little too loudly, "Nice seeing you, Ned. You come by later if you need anything."

She released Ned and squeezed herself back behind her food stall, and Ned and Josephine walked away, waving casually as they went. "That was lucky," Ned mumbled. "She's so smitten with my father, she won't tell anyone she saw you." They walked out of the market and onto a broader street.

Josephine was confused. "But what about your mother?"

When he spoke, Ned's voice was strained. "She left us a long time ago."

There was an awkward silence until Josephine blurted, "My mother's gone too."

"Really?" Ned replied. He was the only child he knew who didn't have a mother.

"She died." Josephine wasn't sure she had ever said that out loud before. She and her father had never spoken about her mother after she'd gone.

"What happened?" Ned asked.

"She got sick. Pneumonia."

"Wow. That's even worse than mine leaving." He said this and then immediately regretted it. "Sorry."

"No, it's okay. I was young. I barely remember her."

"But you've still got your father, right? He must be worried sick about you," Ned said matter-of-factly.

Josephine frowned. She wondered if her father *was* worried. How long had it taken him to even notice she was missing? Her deepest fear was that he was relieved she was gone. "Where are we going?" she asked, suddenly wanting to change the subject.

Ned pointed to a dark alley leading off the main

street, and Josephine felt her nerve starting to waver. She could only hope that *this* time she was trusting the right person. This was her last chance to run away. But where in the world to?

TWENTY-SIX

The Master wore an oily, sinister grin and picked at a cold piece of goose on the table.

Fargus felt the anger rise from his center. All his life he had suppressed the hatred inside himself, hatred for the unknown man who had taken his family away. As Fargus stared at this pint-size boy, he began to see a blinding white. He jumped from his seat and raced for the Master's throat. The servants were upon him in seconds and the Master laughed. "Ha! Well done! Exactly as I would have done it." He dabbed at the corners of his mouth with a napkin. "We really must work on your rage, Fargus." Fargus struggled to free himself from the two servants. "I know you are angry with me—in fact, you probably blame all of your problems on me—but let's be honest, shall we? Why is it that my ship went adrift? Was it my fault? Or someone else's? In fact, Fargus, wasn't it *your* fault?"

Fargus stopped struggling. *He knows? How could he know?*

As if reading his mind, the Master said, "I told you. I know everything that happens within my domain. And anyone that looks at you can see the guilt that lurks behind those soppy brown eyes. Would you like to scream, Fargus? I mean, *really* scream? Why don't you give it a go?" Fargus stared daggers at him.

The Master gave a signal to one of the servants, who grabbed a candle and brought it near. Another servant grabbed Fargus's arm and forced him to hold out his left hand. The man holding the candle brought it closer, dipping the flame beneath Fargus's exposed palm.

As the flame got closer, Fargus tried to ignore the pain and keep a stony expression; he was determined to defy the Master. But soon he felt as if his whole hand were on fire, and he could actually smell his flesh beginning to burn. It was unbearable.

And then he couldn't hold it in anymore.

He opened his mouth and screamed. The sound that emerged was barely human; it was deep and guttural and could have come only from the throat of someone who hadn't made a sound in five years. "Gggguuuaaaahhhrrrggg!" Once he started, he couldn't stop. He was sickened that the Master knew his horrible secret but also relieved to finally be able to let it out—the years of pent-up anger and self-loathing.

The Master grinned. "I think we could do some great things together, Fargus," he said. "We have more in common than you realize."

Tears streamed down Fargus's face.

"Let me put it another way. If you decide to work for me, then I shall tell you where your parents are. Sound fair?"

He nodded. Anything to stop the pain.

At the Master's signal the servant removed the candle from under Fargus's hand. "And enough of this nodding and shaking. I think it is time you spoke."

Fargus's eyes rolled back in his head as he tried to ignore the pain and focus on what the Master was saying.

"What you lack is . . . motivation. I know! That smelly girl you came here with. Ida, I believe her name is. For every sentence you speak, you shall add one day to her life."

Fargus struggled against his captors, but the servants tightened their grips and kept him firmly in place.

"Oh, but it's so easy. And a good bargain, in my opinion. So let's try again. Do you want your friend to live?"

Fargus leaned over as if he was going to be sick. His

hand throbbed and he could feel the blisters forming already. He coughed and spit, trying to clear his throat. He opened his mouth but nothing came out. He tried again and produced a retching sound. On the third try, he felt the sound rising from his belly, riding up his throat and creeping over his tongue. "Yesssss."

It didn't quite sound like a word—it was more of a primitive shriek—but the Master clapped with pleasure. "Well done, boy! I had a feeling you would see it my way." He clapped twice more and Mr. Seaworthy reappeared.

"Take the boy upstairs to one of the private rooms and give him a bath . . . maybe two. And find some salve for that hand." He turned to Fargus. "I shall be calling for you soon, boy. And if you are considering escape, feel free, and if you manage to succeed, then you can live out the rest of your miserable life wondering what happened to your beloved family. Good day."

The Master waved them away.

Mr. Seaworthy led Fargus out the door, putting a withered arm over Fargus's shoulder as they walked down the hall. "Don't worry, son. I've been with the Master for twenty years and now it just seems like any other job. You'll get used to it." Fargus looked down at his burned hand, feeling the terrible, sharp pain throbbing up his arm, and he highly doubted that would be true.

TWENTY-SEVEN

Ned stopped in front of a simple door, removed a key from around his neck, and proceeded to unlock a series of hidden and complicated locks. Josephine felt her heart beat faster.

Ned opened the door and revealed a small apartment. He ushered Josephine inside, and she was pleasantly surprised by the warm, inviting room that lay within.

The space was compact but filled to the brim. It was cluttered and yet suggested some kind of order. There were the essentials: two small beds and night tables, candles for reading, a few chairs, a stove, and a tiny kitchen with a sink and table. She also saw several chessboards, their pieces frozen in the middle of various games. There was a woodworking corner with knives, rulers, and shavings all over the floor, and there were gadgets in another corner: a microscope, a telescope, and something that Josephine didn't recognize, a long brass tube with clocks attached to it.

But the most amazing thing to Josephine was the sheer number of books. They lined each wall and were stuffed into every available crevice. She scanned the titles: There were old books and new ones, true stories and fantasies. There were books on science and math and physics and philosophy. Josephine found her head spinning. All she wanted to do was sit in the armchair and read every last one of them.

Ned was busy taking off his dirty boots, so she approached a precariously high stack of leather-bound volumes and turned her head sideways so she could read the titles. She was intrigued by one called *The Philosophy of Time Travel* and reached out for it when a voice emerged from the kitchen, startling her.

"I wouldn't touch that if I were you."

Josephine snapped her head around to see a tall, lean man with the same large forehead and kind smile as Ned standing next to the kitchen table.

"The whole thing's liable to go over, and if you're lying under a pile of books, I won't be able to ask your name."

Josephine stepped away from the books. "I'm Josephine."

The man limped toward Josephine and slowly squatted down to her height. Josephine thought the man looked much too young to be hobbling around. He had sandy brown hair and a huge Adam's apple that bobbed up and down when he talked.

"Hello," he said in a warm voice. "My name is Morgan. I'm Ned's father." He put his hand on Josephine's shoulder. "Ned, why is she all wet?"

Ned became a bit sheepish. "She was all dopey from something Alma and Bruce gave her, so I . . . uh . . . threw her into the Cherry Spring."

Morgan stood and snatched a blanket from one of the beds. He wrapped it around Josephine and offered her a seat on the bed. "This will keep you warm until I get the fire going." An amused expression on his face, he chided his son, "You know, making her chew on a blue thistle would have had the same effect." He looked at Josephine. "You will have to excuse Ned. He never had any patience for herbology."

Ned scowled and sat in a chair opposite Josephine as Morgan began to pack kindling into the wood-burning stove. "So what brings you to Gulm?"

Josephine hesitated. She wanted to trust this man—Ned, too—but after what had happened with Alma and Bruce, she wasn't sure how much she should reveal.

Morgan seemed to read her thoughts. "No matter. What's important is that you're safe now." He expertly lit the fire and shut the iron door. "So where are the others?"

Ned answered before Josephine had the chance. "Alma and Bruce gave them to the Master!"

Josephine burst out, "You don't know that! Ida and Fargus might have just run away! They might be out in the forest right now!"

Ned looked at Josephine as a doctor might look at a delusional patient. "Yeah, well, they were gone when I got there."

"Hmm." Morgan shook his head. "I'm very sorry to hear that."

"Why is it so awful? Who is the Master? What will he do to them? Why won't anyone answer my questions?!" Josephine was frantic and her face had turned hot and red. She was so frustrated, she began to cry.

Ned panicked, not sure how to deal with the emotions of a girl.

Morgan, having more experience, sat down next to her on the bed and put an arm around her shoulder. "It's all right. Everything's going to be okay."

Josephine tried to stop crying, but despite her best efforts, the little choked sobs kept coming. She was crying for Ida and Fargus, for herself for being in this strange land, but soon she was mostly crying because she couldn't remember the last time her own father had put an arm around her.

"Would you like some hot tea?" he offered.

She sniffled and shrugged.

Morgan stood and went to the stove. Josephine wiped her eyes, a little embarrassed, but felt much better now that she had let everything out.

Ned leaned forward in his seat, gaping at her. "You don't know who the Master is?" This was a completely foreign idea to him, having known about the Master since the day he was born. "Unbelievable."

Morgan, ignoring Ned's shock, said, "You must have traveled from quite a distance if word of the Master never reached you."

"Yes, I think I did," Josephine answered. Morgan almost remarked on this strange reply but then chose not to. "Now, will you please answer my questions?"

"Have some tea," Morgan said, handing her a cup. "Relax now, and I'll tell you what I can."

Josephine set the tea aside. Never again would she drink something offered to her by a stranger. Ned took his happily and began to gulp it down.

Morgan sat in a large rocking chair—obviously his favorite spot, since the cushion held a permanent mold of his backside—and reached into his vest pocket, pulling out a pouch of tobacco and some rolling papers. He began to roll a cigarette, methodical and precise, and Josephine watched as he made it tighter and tighter between his fingers. She felt she might burst if he didn't start explaining soon. He licked the paper and secured it, forming a cigarette no fatter than a toothpick, then found matches in his vest and struck one upon his boot. As he lit the cigarette and unbuttoned his vest, he began to speak.

TWENTY-EIGHT

When I was boy, I thought this place was heaven. My family lived on a farm on the outskirts of Gulm. My father wasn't one for education, so we didn't get to school very often. Mostly, we helped work the farm. We milked the cows and gathered eggs. I would work in the fields during harvest time. My mother was afraid we'd grow up ignorant, so she started sneaking us books."

"'Us'?" Josephine inquired.

"Me and my sister, Lucy. She was eight years younger than I was, so in a lot of ways I raised her. Showed her the best swimming spots, taught her how to read. She didn't like reading much. She just kept reading one book over and over again. It was called *The Dancing Possum*. Lucy thought the idea of a possum dancing was the funniest thing she'd ever heard. She made up a little dance, and every night after supper we would beg her to do 'the dancing possum.'" He smiled, recalling that happy time long ago, but then his face grew dark.

"And then the war came. Gulm had the misfortune of being between two lands that hated each other, and our town seemed like the perfect stronghold for each one. We were a simple people with simple ideas, and few of us knew anything about war. We had no weapons to speak of, no strategies.

"I hid with my family in a cellar near our farm for more than a year while the two rival armies took turns storming Gulm. Cut off from trade with other towns and nearly out of food, my father and I would sneak out at night and hunt in the forest. One week the only thing we could find was a possum. I shot it through the heart with an arrow. I'll never forget Lucy's face when we brought it home. In one single moment, we'd taken away her childhood."

For a moment Morgan fell silent, and Josephine watched as his cigarette became small enough to singe his fingers. He stubbed it out and continued, "One day we went outside, and to our amazement all the soldiers were gone. They'd left overnight, as suddenly as they'd arrived. At first we thought that divine fortune had smiled on us, and we celebrated. But the day the soldiers left was the beginning of a much darker time.

"A boy arrived. He walked to the center of the town square and announced that he was responsible for winning the war and that from that day forward we would be required to pay homage to him. At first we laughed, thought he was a fool, until he introduced us to the Brothers. The boy explained that the Brothers were under his command, and his command alone. He would instruct them to protect our city, if we obeyed him, but if we chose not to, he would order them to destroy us. Once we realized that he was serious, that he had us under his control, we had no choice. He began to demand tributes."

"What kind of tributes? Money?"

"No. Giving him money would've left Gulm its soul. The boy took the thing he knew would bring us to our knees."

Ned finished for him. "He took the children."

Josephine felt a chill run up her spine. "All of them? Everybody?"

Morgan shook his head. "It was one from each family. And if anyone refused, the Master said he would send the Brothers to kill the remaining children. We had a week to comply.

"Gulm became as silent as the inside of a coffin. No one went outside. I don't think anyone even ate. We were full of fear and anger and shame. I'd just turned eighteen, so I was immune. I've never hated a birthday more than that one. If I'd been younger, I could've gone in Lucy's place.

"My family knew we would never sacrifice Lucy, so my father and I planned our escape—he collected food and I tried to make us warmer clothes—while my mother spoiled Lucy with all her favorite games and sweets. We knew other families would be trying to flee and that most of them would head east to the plains or south to the lakes. So we decided to head north, to the glaciers.

"On the third day we made our move. Under the cover of darkness we left behind the farm and headed into the forest, taking only what we could carry. We walked day and night, never stopping. We took turns carrying Lucy. We tried to lie to her, to tell her that all families dreamed of moving north and that we were leaving the farm behind of our own desire. But she knew. She was always sharp as a thorn. But she played along with us. And as we walked, we'd talk about the home we would build of ice, and the seals we would keep as pets. After the sixth day I began to believe it myself, and I even found myself smiling at the idea of my father ice fishing.

"My parents decided we needed to have a proper rest and a decent meal. So we stopped for a night. We found a concealed spot among the trees, and I hunted pheasants for dinner. Mother made a fire and we ate and listened to my father talk about his days as a 'bear wrestler.' My mother howled with laughter and told us the closest thing to a bear he'd ever wrestled was the rug in her mother's house. Lucy laughed and laughed and my father pretended to be very angry with my mother. That night we fell asleep full of hope. But when we woke, Lucy was gone.

"At first I thought she'd wandered off, looking for water or something, anything. But I knew. I knew the Brothers had been there. I could smell them."

Josephine felt tears running down her cheeks, wondering if Fargus and Ida were doomed to the same fate as Lucy. "And you never saw her again?"

"No. We hurried back to Gulm looking for her, but we were told that the Master had sold all the children into slavery, in order to pay for his army."

"That savage!" Josephine blurted out.

"The townspeople were determined to find out where the children had been sent. The Master had taken over a large estate in the western district, and a group of us decided to storm his manor with the weapons we had: axes, shovels, and knives. At dawn, my father led me and the other men of Gulm up the hill and past the gates of the estate. But the Brothers were waiting. They attacked us at once, killing dozens of men in the blink of an eye—they were merciless and unrelenting. I was one of the lucky ones. They broke my leg and left me for dead. I crawled for two days to get back home. Most of the others, my father included, never returned."

Josephine could almost taste the dark pain that now permeated the room. Morgan continued, "Since then, no one has had the nerve to confront the Master and he hasn't set foot outside of his manor."

There was a long silence. Josephine hesitated before asking, "What about Ned? Does the Master want him, too?"

"The Master demanded the children nearly twenty years ago and hasn't asked for any since. But with the disappearance of Ida and Fargus . . . well, I don't know what to think."

"He's been taking kids from the Institute all this time. Ida told me."

Morgan was surprised at the news. He rubbed his chin. "Orphans? Hmm. That makes sense. He wouldn't have to worry about vengeful parents, then, would he?"

"But the Institute is empty now. Ida and Fargus were the only ones left."

Ned asked his father, "Does that mean the Master will want more kids from Gulm?" He was trying to put on a brave face, but his voice betrayed fear.

"Don't you worry about it, Ned. I'll never let him take you."

"But what could we do if—"

"Enough!" Morgan thundered. "You must trust me, Ned. I will NEVER let him take you."

Josephine wished someone felt that deeply about protecting her. "Morgan, what *are* the Brothers?"

"That's a very good question. And it's why I have all of these. . . ." He waved to his collection of books on biology and animal species. "But I have yet to read anything about them specifically. It's as if they never existed until now. All I know is that they are seen only during the day, they have no mouths, and they smell like the dead. They are . . . a mystery."

Josephine asked a question she wasn't sure she wanted answered. "Why did the Jarvises give Ida and Fargus to the Master but not me?"

She saw Morgan's large forehead crease. "I'm not sure."

"I have a guess," Ned offered. Both Morgan and Josephine looked at him in surprise. "Dad, ask Josephine what her last name is."

Morgan raised an eyebrow. "Her last name?"

"Russing," Josephine offered. "So what?"

Morgan rubbed his chin again, but Ned answered her, excited to share the information. "They say the Master is from a dynasty in Drubshire, and before anyone called him the Master, he was named Leopold Reginald Russing. His family is rich and cruel, and—"

"Ned. That's enough," Morgan said sternly. He could see Ned's words were upsetting Josephine, who looked positively gray. "I'm sure the name Russing is just a coincidence," he added supportively.

But it was not just the name *Russing* that had knocked the breath out of Josephine. Her distress was caused by the fact that Leopold Reginald Russing was also the full name of her father. Mr. Russing had never been popular in her town, but she'd always assumed it was because of his gloves. What if there was more? What if her father was somehow involved with the Master and all the missing children? Or worse, what if he *was* the Master? Josephine felt woozy.

"I think Alma and Bruce must have known how valuable she was," Ned told his father, "and maybe they were going to try to get big money for her!"

"Whether it involved money or not, I'm sure the Jarvises knew the significance of the name." He looked at Josephine again. "The more I hear, the more I'm starting to believe you're here for a reason."

"No! There is no reason!" she exclaimed. "It was a mistake, an accident. And I just want to go back home!" She missed her room, her school, and Ms. Kirdle more than ever. She missed feeling safe and warm in her bed. And now, more than anything, she wanted to rush back to her father and demand to know if he had anything to do with the Master or the evil Russing dynasty.

"Please! Please help me find a way home!" she pleaded.

"Now, now," Morgan soothed. "Don't get upset. You'll make yourself ill. What you need is a good night's sleep. And in the morning we'll come up with a plan."

Ned said excitedly, "A plan for what?"

"For getting Josephine back to where she belongs."

These were the best words she'd ever heard. Josephine wanted to hug them both. "Thank you!"

"Ned, fix us some dinner. As for me, I think I have some reading to do."

TWENTY-NINE

A clamor came from the Jarvis home. Alma was extremely agitated, cursing under her breath as she prepared dinner. She had been yelling for more than an hour. Bruce sat at the table, resigned to listening to his wife until she ran out of steam.

"And now the whole town knows that we let her get away! You were asked to do one thing, ONE THING, and you couldn't do it. All you had to do was keep an eye on her. How hard could it be? She had enough drugs in her to incapacitate three people! But oh no, it's too much to ask Bruce Jarvis to keep a sleepy little girl from running away. We almost had something good happen—a little respect within the community! Can't you do anything right?"

"I just went to fetch some fertilizer," he protested.

"More like you were napping behind the barn!"

"I was gone only a second."

Alma spat, "Just like you were gone only a second when they took Sarah?"

It took Bruce a moment to believe what he'd heard. "What are you saying?"

"I think you know."

"They came in the night . . . we never even saw them . . ."

"You should have protected her! You were her father!"

Bruce's head sagged at the truth of her words. "I thought we were talking about Josephine."

"Get out. Just go. I can't look at you anymore."

"You don't mean that . . . you're just upset. We let the girl get away. So what? What can anyone do? What more can they take from us?"

Alma looked at him with a cold heart and told him to gather his things.

THIRTY

Josephine woke up, not sure where she was. Then, in the dim light, she saw Morgan sitting in his rocking chair, staring at her.

"What's wrong?" she mumbled. "What's happening?"

He whispered so as not to wake Ned. "There's no need to be alarmed. I've just been waiting for you to wake up."

"Why? Have you been there all night?"

"I want to ask you about something you said last night. Do you remember when I said you must have traveled from quite a distance and you said, 'I think I did'?"

"Yes."

"Why aren't you sure?"

Josephine lay back down and considered how she

should answer. "I suppose you could say that the way I got here . . . to Gulm . . . was very . . . uh . . . unusual."

"Unusual how?"

"I fell into a . . . a . . . hole or passageway or something—I'm not sure I want to talk about it."

"I knew it!" His eyes flared with excitement, and he leaned in. "Josephine, for my entire life I've heard stories about passageways, doors, tunnels, whatever you want to call them, that connect different places. They can transport a person to a new land, a new time, or even a different dimension. Legend has it that these tunnels are strongly linked to a person's subconscious desires. I think that's what happened to you."

Josephine felt a flutter of hope, as if she'd been speaking a foreign language all this time and had finally found a translator.

Morgan stood up with the help of his cane, his excitement growing. "I've spent fifteen years searching for such a tunnel. As soon as Ned was born, I knew we needed to leave Gulm, but the Brothers have kept us from escaping. Maybe the tunnel you're describing could take us to safety!"

"But how do you know these tunnels aren't dangerous? I landed in Gulm, even though I didn't want to."

"Are you sure you didn't want to? What were you thinking about right before you came through?"

Josephine tried to remember. "I was looking for Fargus, and I was trying to figure out where he was."

"So at that moment, would you say your primary goal was to find your friend?"

"Yes. I guess I would."

"Well, don't you see? The tunnel took you where you needed to go to find him. You *did* want to come here!"

Morgan was right. At that moment in the shed, she *had* wanted nothing more than to find Fargus.

"I have something you may find interesting," Morgan said. He began searching through his shelves of books. "Every so often I come across a mention of the tunnels in our stories and histories." He pulled down a thick volume of local myths. It was Josephine's favorite kind of book, extremely heavy and bound in aging leather. Morgan flipped through the yellowing pages, detonating a large puff of dust. "I think this one is my favorite," he said, coughing.

He handed the book to Josephine and pointed to a dog-eared page. She got up out of her cozy bed and sat on top of the blankets. The book was almost too heavy for her to lift, so she laid it on her lap.

Morgan explained, "I used to read it to Neddy when he was younger."

She nodded and began to read.

BROKHUN'S CRACKS

For many centuries the Dark World was ruled by King Brokhun. He was cruel and caused much suffering throughout the land. He had no affection for any creature except himself. This included his wife, the ogress Ladona. One day Ladona gave birth to a daughter, Angrin, and when Brokhun set eyes upon the newborn, love finally filled his heart. He spoiled the child and never let her out of his sight. While she was with him, every living creature in the universe experienced a golden age, with plentiful food, long life, and abundant love.

As Angrin grew older, though, she became afraid of the evil creatures that roamed the Dark World, terrified that one day they would eat her. So she ran away. Brokhun was brokenhearted, and he searched the entire universe for her. When he could not find her, he fell to the ground and wept, pounding his fists mightily upon the earth. His pounding shook the land and the seas and the skies. On the fourth day of his mourning, Brokhun pounded so hard he cracked open the universe, creating passageways between all worlds.

Brokhun declared that the passageways, thenceforth known as Brokhun's Cracks, would remain open until he was reunited with his dear Angrin.

Josephine closed the book, wrinkled her nose, and peered at Morgan. "Do you believe that story?"

"It's a nice story, don't you think? But no, I can't say that I believe in Brokhun. I'm a man of science, not myth, and in physics there has long been a theory about something similar to his cracks called a *wormhole*."

"A wormhole? What's that?"

"Think of time and space . . . as an apple." He grabbed an apple out of the kitchen and a pencil to demonstrate. "Now, imagine a worm crawling around this apple. Normally he would have to travel the entire circumference to get around it, but what if he suddenly decided to take a shortcut by burrowing his way through the center?" Morgan shoved the pencil through the apple until Josephine could see the lead tip come out the other end. "The worm has created one of your passages. The idea is that space and time—say, the meat and juice of the apple—are one and the same."

Morgan could see Josephine was confused. "Don't be embarrassed if you don't understand. Very few people do." Morgan came to sit beside her. "So where was *your* wormhole, Josephine?"

"I don't know where it was, exactly. One minute I was in my shed at home and the next thing I knew I was in the cellar of the Higgins Institute for Wayward

Children and Forsaken Youth. And no matter where I looked, I couldn't find the way back."

"The passageways are probably hidden very well. If they were in plain sight and everyone used them, there would be chaos. The time/space continuum would likely collapse in on itself." He shuddered at the thought.

Josephine asked, "The time/space con—what?" Her molars ached from all the new information.

"Don't worry about it. The important thing is that I think I have what we need." He crossed the room and picked up the strange little instrument with the clocks that Josephine had noticed earlier. It was about a foot long, and Morgan held it out horizontally for her to inspect. The stem was made of tubular brass and on each end the metal curved up and was topped by a small timepiece a little larger than the face of a wristwatch.

"I've been working on this for some time. I call it a *claganmeter*. Imagine that I were holding two stethoscopes and I could listen to your heartbeat and Ned's heartbeat at the same time. I could tell you if there was a difference between the two, even if it was minuscule. Well, the claganmeter does the same thing, but it measures time at two locations simultaneously."

"Measures time, like a watch?" Josephine asked, not sure what was so impressive.

"Yes . . . and no. This has two timepieces and can tell

me if there is a difference in time between point A and point B."

"That's silly. How could two spaces that are only inches apart have different times?"

"Exactly. Normally, they shouldn't. So if we move the claganmeter around this room"—he began to walk around the living room holding the instrument horizontally, so that the clocks were on either side of him—"everywhere we go, the two clocks read the same time. But if we went to that cellar, the place where you first arrived, I bet you we would find an area where the clocks tell us two different times." He paused and added triumphantly, "And *that's* how we'll know where the door is!"

"The door?"

"The wormhole! Because the passage itself leads to another time and place, it is inevitable that some of that time inconsistency has leaked into our world, like the juice, say, leaking from the apple."

"But how do you know it works?" she asked, curiosity piqued.

"He doesn't," came a voice from the other bed.

Morgan and Josephine saw that Ned was awake and had been listening for some time. Ned rolled his eyes at his father. "He's been trying to use that thing for five years now."

"Yes, but Neddy, don't you see? We weren't looking in

the right place! This girl can take us to the room where she landed!"

Josephine wrinkled her nose again. "I studied science in school, but we never learned about anything like this. It doesn't really make sense to me."

Ned moaned, "It doesn't make sense to anyone. Never has. Never will." He grumpily rolled back over and pretended to go back to sleep.

Morgan whispered, "Ned doesn't like this subject. His mother and I . . . well . . . she didn't believe in the doors either and we didn't . . . uh . . ."

"She left, Dad—just say she left."

"Yes. She left." Morgan turned a bit red, but then a smile crept back over his mouth. "But, Josephine, don't you see? You're a gift! *You* are what we've been waiting for!" He folded up the claganmeter until it was only about six inches long and turned toward the lump that was Ned. "Ned! Get up. We have to get going."

"Where?" he moaned.

"To the Higgins Institute! To find one of Brokhun's Cracks!"

"Wait!" Josephine cried. "This is all happening too fast."

Morgan was confused. "But I thought you wanted to go home. That's what you told me last night."

"I do. But we can't just leave Ida and Fargus with the

Master. We have to go get them and bring them with us through the wormhole!"

Ned got out of bed. "She's right, Dad. We can't just leave them there."

Morgan sighed. "I wish we could save them. I really do. But in twenty years no one has been able to get into the Master's estate. What can the three of us do? You are only children and I am a pathetic man with a limp."

A sly look appeared on Josephine's face. "You are forgetting one thing."

Ned and Morgan answered together, "What?"

Josephine stood regally and bowed. "*I* am a Russing."

THIRTY-ONE

Josephine's plan began with a letter. Ned supplied her with paper and an ink pen and she used her best handwriting.

Your Excellency, the Master of Gulm,

My name is Josephine Russing and I am a stranger to your land. I have traveled far and heard so much about you. I would be delighted if you would grant me an audience. It is so rare to discover new relatives, and I think it would be great fun to meet each other, don't you?

Sincerely,

Josephine Isabelle Russing

Ned read the letter over her shoulder. "'Great fun'? Have you gone completely barking mad?"

Josephine answered sweetly, "I need to sound harmless and innocent if he's going to let me into his home." Josephine blew on the letter to help the ink dry.

"But why . . . ?" At that moment Ned realized what Josephine had in mind and the two of them grinned at each other mischievously.

Ned handed the letter to Morgan. "It's brilliant. He can't possibly resist."

Morgan read the letter and his jaw dropped. "So you connive your way inside. How does that succeed in doing anything but put you in mortal danger?"

Josephine thought this part of the plan was obvious. "I'll distract the Master while the two of you sneak into the house and find Fargus and Ida."

"First of all, it's hardly a house," Morgan interjected, panicking. "It's a huge manor, with high walls and a deep moat. And second, I'm afraid that I'm useless in such tasks." He tapped his bum leg with his cane. "And I'm hardly letting you and Ned go alone."

"Why not?" Ned demanded. "You've been training me for something like this my whole life! I can swim like a fish and climb like a cat. You taught me!"

"But the Brothers . . ."

"It'll be dark by then. They won't be out!"

"No!" Morgan yelled suddenly. "I won't let it happen again. I won't let the Master have you, too!"

Josephine was frightened by his passion, but Ned was obviously used to it, because he didn't flinch. He walked up to his father and put a hand on his shoulder. "Dad. You raised me to be brave and to do the right thing. And the right thing is to go rescue Ida and Fargus. And you know I'm right."

Morgan sat down in his chair, turning over objections in his mind. He opened his mouth to speak, but— nothing. He sat for several minutes, and Josephine could imagine him bolting the door and never letting Ned outside ever again. When he finally spoke, it was in a whisper. "I will let you go under one condition."

Ned's eyes flashed. "What?"

"After Josephine has had dinner with the Master, regardless of whether or not you have succeeded in rescuing the other children, you will take Josephine straight to the Institute, find the wormhole, and then . . . the two of you will go through it together."

"What!?" Ned was shocked. "I'm not leaving Gulm."

"It is the only way I can keep you from the Master forever. And I'll join you in Josephine's land as soon as I can. That is my condition."

As Ned paced back and forth, Josephine could see his inner turmoil. If he wanted to stay with his father in Gulm, he would have to abandon Josephine and the others to the Master, and he would have to live with that for the rest of his life. But if he went through the wormhole with Josephine, he might never see his father again.

She spoke up. "Can I speak to Ned in private for a moment?"

Ned and Morgan looked up in surprise.

"Sure," Ned said, and pointed to the door. He and Josephine walked out to the alley, out of earshot of the apartment.

"I know your father has put you in a difficult position, but I have to be honest. I don't really think we're going to be able to find one of Brokhun's Cracks anyway. No offense to your father, but I think his theories and his claganmeter are pretty far-fetched."

Ned smiled. "No offense taken. Everyone in town thinks he's crazy."

"Do you?"

"He's not crazy. But he may be a little . . . *optimistic* about the claganmeter."

Josephine nodded in understanding.

"Even if we find the wormhole," Ned added, "I can't go with you. I won't leave him."

"I know that, and you know that, but . . ." Josephine paused. "He doesn't need to know that." She was shocked at her own audacity, but she would do whatever it took to rescue Ida and Fargus.

Ned smiled conspiratorially. "Okay. Let's go back inside."

When they went back in, Morgan was carefully folding Josephine's letter and placing it into an envelope.

"Dad, I'm going with Josephine," Ned announced.

Morgan looked up. "And you agree to leave Gulm with her?"

"Yes." Ned looked away from his father, afraid he might see the lie.

Morgan looked sad but resigned. "Then we must act quickly. First, you should take Josephine's letter to the marketplace and give it to Samuel Fromma. Tell him it must reach the Master immediately. Now, he won't be too keen to go to the manor, so you'd better give him this." Morgan reached into his pocket and retrieved a shiny new coin. Ned took the letter and the coin and then hugged his father, surprising Morgan with the intensity of his emotions.

"Thank you, Father. I won't let you down, I promise."

Morgan choked up and hugged him back, fierce and loving. "Neddy, you could no more let me down than you could change the color of your eyes." He squeezed tightly and then released him. "Get going. And in the meantime I'm going to teach this little lady a few tricks that might come in handy."

"Uh-oh." Ned grinned. "Look out, Josephine. He might just turn you into a warrior." And with that he put on his cap and was out the door.

THIRTY-TWO

Ida slept on and off in her dark prison. She had no idea what day it was. All she knew was blackness. She longed to straighten her legs and arms. She thought of food: sweet lamb chops and roast potatoes and lemon fritters. She could almost taste them. As soon as she had the memory of lemon upon her tongue, she leaned forward and began to bite the ropes around her wrists. She had been gnawing at them little by little. But she could never stand it for more than a few minutes, as the threads absorbed what little moisture she had in her throat.

As she nibbled at the cords, she felt a vibration in her feet. She stopped and concentrated on the energy that crept up her legs. Suddenly a shock ran through her body, making her thrash like a dying fish.

It stopped just as suddenly as it had started and Ida struggled to catch her breath. She didn't know what had happened, but she wasn't sure if she could last much longer.

THIRTY-THREE

Mr. Seaworthy shuffled down the hall with a trembling silver tray full of hot tea, fresh cakes, and a letter that had just arrived for the Master. He tried not to look down at the overfull teapot, knowing that peeking was the quickest path to spilling. The Master was in good spirits today, and Mr. Seaworthy dared not ruin his mood by serving him soggy cakes. Fifteen years before, he had served him soggy cakes and the Master had had him thrown into the moat. Mr. Seaworthy sank to the bottom like a stone and just lay there, calmly waiting to drown. He stayed that way for nearly five minutes, until the Master decided he could, possibly, eat scones instead of the soggy cakes. One of the other servants was ordered to jump into the murky waters and pull Mr. Seaworthy out, and the crooked old man emerged as stoic as ever. This was what had earned him the nickname "Seaworthy." Before the incident his name had been Buttermeyer.

He arrived at the Master's bedchamber and entered without knocking.

"Ah, Seaworthy, it's about time. I'm famished." The Master lay in his enormous bed, wearing silk pajamas and a nightcap, and he happily reached for a cake as soon as Mr. Seaworthy showed him the tray. As he shoved it into his mouth, he opened the letter with sticky fingers.

Mr. Seaworthy walked to the other side of the bed to put down the tray. This took longer that one might have expected, since the bed took up most of the room. Its giant canopy frame was made of mahogany and the sheets of fine silk. Mr. Seaworthy had thought on more than one occasion that the entire staff could have fitted comfortably in the Master's bed. One might have thought that the Master would have rejected such a large piece of furniture since it only served to emphasize his diminutive size, but Mr. Seaworthy suspected that while lying in the bed the Master felt as if he were the captain of an enormous ship.

"Seaworthy! This is incredible; it's the most fabulous stroke of luck!"

"Yes, sir," Mr. Seaworthy agreed, having no idea what the Master was talking about.

"That girl, the one those horrible farmers told me

about, *she* wants to see *me*. Here I thought I was going to have to craft some elaborate scheme to capture her, and instead she is practically surrendering to me! The poor ninny!"

"Yes, sir."

"Lovely cakes. Tell the cook he is using too much vanilla."

"Yes, sir."

"This is a fine day, Seaworthy, a fine day. I am finally going to learn the secret to Brokhun's Cracks. And all of my plans will come to fruition!" Mr. Seaworthy began sweeping up the crumbs that had landed on the Master's sheets with a tiny whisk broom he carried in his coat pocket. "I want to wear something special today. Something dignified and royal that says, 'I will claw your eyes out for fun.'"

"I know the suit you mean, sir." Mr. Seaworthy shuffled toward the deep closet and began searching for the perfect ensemble. As he picked out a pair of wee trousers, he considered how much he had aged in the time he had been in the Master's service and how little the Master had changed.

He daydreamed of the day when the Master would rise and ring the breakfast bell and no one would answer. And when the servants were finally sent to find Mr. Seaworthy, they would knock down his door only to find him in bed, no longer breathing, holding a picture of his sweet daughter, Petunia Buttermeyer, whose safety Mr. Seaworthy had insured by his boundless servitude to the Master.

THIRTY-FOUR

Josephine struggled for breath while Morgan spurred her on. "Kick me! Go on. Do it again!"

The two of them stood wide apart in the empty alleyway next to Morgan and Ned's apartment, and once again, Josephine took a running start and attempted to leap in the air and kick Morgan in the chest. But when her heel made contact with him, it was with his hip, not his chest, and the force with which she delivered the blow was as insubstantial as a feather landing on his cheek. She huffed in frustration.

"Now, don't give up. It's about practice. You can't think about your *foot* kicking me—you have to make your *whole body* do the kicking, and your foot just happens to make the first contact. Do you understand?"

Josephine nodded, although she wasn't sure she understood him completely.

She walked away and prepared herself to try it again. First she eyed the point on Morgan's body that she was aiming for, and then she mentally formed a picture of the kind of kick she would use. She breathed in, deeply and slowly, and then, on the exhale, she ran toward him as fast as she could. But she started off on the wrong leg, so by the time she reached him, she needed to kick him with her left foot instead of her right. And she had no coordination with the left leg. Once again, she barely tapped him.

Morgan smiled patiently. "Balance is important, and you must learn to be as strong with your left leg as you are with your right."

"It's no use, Morgan. I'm just not very . . . athletic."

"Nonsense! You're far too young to say what you 'are' or 'are not.' In fact, I am too young to say it too! Perhaps a man who's seconds from dying can make some sort of conclusion about the man that he is, but even then I think it's presumptuous! You've escaped from the Brothers, on foot! You crossed the plains of Gulm, without any food! Then you escaped from the clutches of Bruce and Alma—and now you want to face the Master in person. You are no delicate flower, my dear. You are rugged and brave and you can be as forceful as a tornado if you want."

A tornado. Josephine blushed. No one had ever seen

Josephine as powerful in any way. But as she listened to Morgan, she thought to herself that maybe he was right. She had always felt that there was strength within her, bursting to get out. She'd never known, though, how to tap into it.

"How about this?" He continued with the lesson. "This time, I want you to run toward me and kick me like I'm a locked door that you need to force open."

This image made sense to Josephine. She walked ten paces away, took a deep breath, and pictured herself as a massive tornado capable of flattening a whole town. She exhaled and went running toward Morgan, and this time, as she lifted her leg and bent her knee, she imagined her tornado-self knocking down a door and coming out the other side.

Her foot landed squarely in Morgan's stomach, and Josephine could feel the full force of her body projecting through him. He reeled back in shock, the air knocked out of him. His bad leg collapsed underneath him and he crumpled to the ground.

"Oh, Morgan!" Josephine cried, and ran to him. "I'm sorry! I'm so sorry."

He gulped for air and had to sit still for a few more seconds, but eventually, after he'd caught his breath, he began to laugh. "Yes! That's it. Very good, Josephine!"

"But . . . you aren't mad?"

"Of course not. You did exactly as I taught you." He climbed to his feet and gave her a hug. "You are an excellent pupil, Josephine. And those long legs of yours are going to serve you well."

Josephine marveled at the compliment. She'd always hated her gangly legs, and it had never occurred to her that they would be good for anything.

Just then, Ned rounded the corner. "What's going on?"

Morgan grinned at him. "I was just teaching Josephine a few tactical moves. How did it go?"

"Well, the message was sent by horseback and the Master replied immediately. I was a bit shocked how fast."

Morgan was startled. "You mean, he's already answered? Let me see th—!"

Josephine interrupted. "I wrote the letter. I think I should get to see first."

"Fair enough," Morgan agreed, and Ned handed Josephine the letter. It was in a sealed envelope with a fancy seal stamped in wax.

As Josephine held the letter, she suddenly got very afraid. This was no longer just an idea; it was real. The Master knew about her and had written to her. She had no idea what might be in store for her.

She broke the seal and pulled out the letter, which was written on heavy parchment paper.

Dear Josephine Russing,

*The Master is delighted to have
a relative in his domain, and he
respectfully requests your presence
at his home for dinner and coffee.
Please arrive promptly at seven o'clock.
No guests.*

Sincerely,

Mr. Seaworthy

Attaché to the Master

Josephine, wide-eyed, handed the invitation to Morgan. It had worked.

Morgan sensed her concern. "It's not too late, Josephine. We can still take you to the Institute and get you back home."

She shook her head. "No! I'm going through with our plan. If Ned is still willing." She looked at Ned, her eyes forming a soft plea.

"Of course I'm still in."

Relieved, Josephine smiled. "But the invitation says seven o'clock! How will we get there in time?"

Morgan studied the invitation again. "I know some-one who might be able to help us."

Morgan tottered off to find transportation, leaving

Ned and Josephine alone in the apartment to get ready to leave. Ned packed a bag while Josephine kept practicing her new kick in a mirror. She was amazed that it was her in the reflection. Her cheeks were flushed and her eyes were electric. Her hair was out of her face and the concentration the exercise required gave her a fierce look, like one of the heroines in her books.

After a while she got winded and went to the kitchen for a glass of water. She drank it down in one gulp, and when she looked up, she found Ned staring at her, a strange expression on his face.

"What?" she asked.

"What's it feel like?"

"What's what feel like?"

"Passing through a magic door."

"Oh. Well . . . there's not much to describe, really. It felt like I was falling for a really long time, and a bit like my insides were on my outside, if that makes any sense, and then I landed. And that was it."

"Do people look the same as we do where you come from? Or do they look funny?"

"What are you saying? That *I* look funny?" Josephine felt her new confidence melt away.

"No! No." Ned shook his head. "That's not what I meant. Not at all."

"Then what did you mean?"

"I . . . uh . . ."

Luckily for him, at that very moment the door burst open and Morgan entered wearing a huge grin. "I think I have the answer to our problem."

And from behind him, Beatrice the fruit seller wobbled in, beaming with pleasure. "I'm so happy I could be of help!"

Ned cried, "Oh no, Dad, not her!"

His father shot him a withering look. "Don't be rude, Ned. Miss Beatrice has taken time from her day to help us. Why don't you make her a nice cup of tea?" His eyes dared Ned to argue. So Ned trudged to the kitchen area and began to fill the kettle.

"And this is Josephine," Morgan said to Beatrice.

"Why, of course. So pleased to see you again, dear."

Josephine attempted a small curtsy, because in all her favorite books the well-bred girls always curtsied.

"Isn't she delicious!" Beatrice exclaimed, a comment that, considering this woman's girth, made Josephine uncomfortable. "Come outside with me, dear."

She led Josephine outside, and standing there were two stately-looking horses.

Beatrice pointed to the smaller one, which was a luxurious reddish brown. "Now, this is Mabel, and she's the best size for you, sweetie."

Horses! Josephine couldn't believe it.

"You know how to ride, don't you?"

Josephine shook her head. She had always wanted to learn, but her father, of course, had never taken the time to teach her.

"Well, there's nothing to it. Mabel is well trained. You pull back on her reins when you want to stop, and you give her a kick with your heel when you want to go. You pull her head gently to the right or the left if you need to turn. What could be simpler than that?"

"But how do I make her go faster?" Josephine asked, her voice trembling from excitement.

"Let's make sure you can stay on her before we teach you how to canter," Beatrice replied, but Josephine could tell from her smile that she liked Josephine's gumption.

"Let's see you get up on her," Beatrice ordered. "You need to lift your left foot as high as you can so you reach that stirrup." Josephine did as she was told and she was just barely tall enough to make it. Once she had her left foot in the stirrup, Beatrice said, "Now, hold on to the horn with your left hand and hoist yourself up and over."

"But not too far, Josephine," Morgan warned from the doorway. "Or you'll go tumbling over the other side."

"Leave her alone, Morgan. She's not a moron." Beatrice signaled to Josephine to get on the mare, so Josephine took a firm grip of the horn, the nubby bit at the front of the saddle, lifted herself up, and swung her right leg up and over Mabel. And the next thing she knew, she was sitting on top of a horse!

"She's a natural!" Beatrice exclaimed.

"How's it feel up there?" Morgan inquired.

"Great!" Josephine was ecstatic. She liked how tall the horse made her. She felt powerful.

Just then Ned emerged with his bag and Beatrice's cup of tea, and when he spotted the horses, he exclaimed, "Whoa! Is one of those for me?"

Morgan nodded.

"Fantastic!" Ned cried, shoving Beatrice's tea into her hands and then leaping onto the other horse, a big black stallion. "He's a brute! What's his name?"

"I call him Thistle."

"Thistle? You've got to be kidding!"

"Ned!" Morgan warned.

Ned took the disgust out of his voice. "I just mean . . . he's such a big, powerful horse. Shouldn't he have a big, power-ful name? Like . . . *Thunder*?"

"You can call him whatever you want, young man, but he's going to *answer* to Thistle." Beatrice approached the beautiful horse. "Isn't that right, boy?" She stroked his long nose and scratched behind his ears. "I've raised both these horses from colts, so when you let them go, they'll come straight home to me." She looked at Morgan and added,

"Believe me, I make a cozy home to come home to."

Morgan turned beet red and cleared his throat. "Umm . . . all right, then." He turned back to the children. "Are you two ready to go?"

Josephine nodded, and Ned lifted a bag to show his father, which was packed with food, water, and, most important, the claganmeter.

"You remember how to use it?"

Ned rolled his eyes. "I've watched you do it only a million times, Dad."

Morgan then approached Josephine. "I've got something I want to give you." He took a locket attached to a long gold chain from his coat pocket. "This belonged to my mother. I don't have any daughters to give it to, so . . ." He trailed off, growing embarrassed by his own gesture. He placed the locket in Josephine's small hand.

She opened it and found two pictures, a teenage boy and a young girl, both with sandy brown hair and freckles.

"That's me and my sister, Lucy," Morgan explained.

"I love it," Josephine said, taking the necklace and slipping it over her head. "I'll treasure it. Thank you for everything."

"Don't thank me now. Thank me when I see you back in your land."

She felt teary at the thought of saying good-bye.

"I want you to take this, Neddy," Morgan said, reaching under the back of his coat and pulling out a small dagger sheathed in a shiny green metal.

"But that's your lucky hunting knife!"

"Exactly. And I want all of my luck to be with you kids. Don't be afraid to use this, Neddy. The Master won't show mercy, so neither can you."

Ned's face betrayed fear for the first time. He took the knife and slid it into the back of his pants, wearing it just as his father had. Morgan reached out his hand and Ned shook it, feeling like a man for the first time in his life.

Morgan finally pulled away. "You best be going. You can't be late." He was beginning to choke up, so he pulled out a handkerchief and pretended to blow his nose.

Beatrice put a tender hand on his shoulder. "They'll be fine, dear. You'll see."

"Forward, Thunder!" Ned ordered, but the stallion refused to move.

Josephine clucked her tongue at Mabel, as she had seen people do at home, and the mare clopped past Ned. Josephine turned around to see Ned glaring at his horse, and she chided him, "His name is Thistle."

"Forward, *Thistle*," Ned said grudgingly, nudging the horse forward with the heel of his shoe. Thistle trotted forward and soon caught up to Josephine.

Beatrice and Morgan chuckled as they watched the two of them ride away, but their laughter was tinged with uncertainty and fear.

THIRTY-FIVE

Ida had finally managed to chew through the ropes binding her hands. In the tight space it was very difficult to bend, but after considerable effort she was finally able to reach the ropes around her ankles and slowly work the knots loose. She wiggled her toes and enjoyed the sensation of pins prickling her legs as they woke up. She twisted her torso and crawled into a new position where she could look upward. She saw there was a long passageway with a dim light at the end.

She cleared the hair from her eyes, rubbed her hands together, and spit twice for luck. She then began to climb up the narrow tunnel. The walls were made of dirt and thick tree roots. She clung to the roots, but as her feet searched for a stronghold, she kicked away big chunks of earth and sent herself falling back to the bottom. She tried again. She jumped up, grabbed a root, and pulled up her bruised body. She knew she just needed to get above the level of crumbling dirt. She kicked up her leg even to where her hands were and found support on one of the thicker roots. She heaved herself up until she was squatting and looked skyward for the next sturdy root. She grabbed it and used the same method as before. Again and again she hoisted up her body, all the while trying not to look down at the abyss that threatened to reclaim her.

Her eyes were full of soil and she was dizzy from lack of food. As she neared the opening, she felt she couldn't possibly go any farther. She paused and caught her breath, trying to imagine reaching the top and at last gulping the fresh air. The thought was enticing but not enough to give her hands the motivation to reach up once again. She thought of the Institute, of her family, and then of Fargus. Who would take care of him? No one could understand him but her. Without her he would be forever trapped in silence, and they would drag him away to a house for stupid people. She looked up at the bright light and kept climbing, her heart and head full of thoughts of Fargus. "He'd better appreciate what I've been through for him. If he doesn't, I'll punch the little freak."

She reached the top of the pit and, with one last mighty effort, threw her tired body over the edge. She lay there panting, unable to move, covered in muck and sweat. She didn't think she'd ever been happier to see the sun in her life, although she did wish she had a cool glass of water. She rolled over to take in her surroundings and found she was lying in the middle of a field with no crops, just dirt and tree stumps. There was a foul smell in the air that reminded her of the time she'd hidden strawberries under her bed and then forgotten about them. The Brothers could not be far. The thought was enough to push her to her feet. She had no time to waste resting.

A large manor stood next to the field. It had several towers and a door so large that she figured it must be a drawbridge. Despite the ornate decorations on the front of the house, it had a sad quality to it, as if no one had remembered its birthday for several centuries. Whoever was inside had been responsible for putting her in that hole. Instinctively, Ida set off in the opposite direction of the manor.

She had walked about five yards when she tripped and almost fell into another hole. She cursed to herself, and stood back up. She resumed walking, but soon she heard a voice, faint and very high but definitely a human voice, coming from deep inside this new hole. She went back, got on her knees, and peered down into the blackness.

"Hello?" she asked. No reply. She spoke again but much louder. "HELLO!"

"Who's there?" the tiny voice asked.

"This is Ida. Who's there?"

"Clarence."

"Hello, Clarence. It's nice to meet you."

Up from the hole came a faint "It's nice to meet you, too."

There was an awkward pause. Finally Ida spoke again. "Do you want some help?"

"Uh . . . with what?"

"Getting out of this hole?"

"Oh. I'm not sure."

"Criminy. Is *everyone* around here crazy?"

"What are you doing?"

"Well, at the moment it appears I'm wasting my time talking to some nutter down a hole. But after this, I plan to go to Gulm and find my friend Fargus."

"Ooooh, Gulm. Yes, I'd like that, please."

"Just my luck. The one place he'd like to go," she whispered to herself, rolling her eyes.

"Can you help me out?" Clarence asked.

"I'm not sure. Are your hands tied?"

"Yes."

"Well then, I don't know how you can crawl out."

"Can you untie my hands, please?"

"I just got out of my own hole!"

"Please?"

"Hot maggot breath! I'm on my way."

She found the climb down quite easy, and she had no problems undoing Clarence's ropes. As she untied him, she explained to him how to use the roots to pull himself up the tunnel, and he scurried up with much less effort than she had. As she panted and gasped for air on the climb back up, Clarence helped her with the final pull. She lay on the ground, glaring at his smiling face. He had big green eyes and was probably only seven years old.

"I don't suppose you have any food?" she inquired.

"Sure I do. Everyone prepares sustenance for time in the holes."

Sustenance? What kind of little kid says "sustenance"? Ida wondered.

He reached into his pocket and pulled out a squashed ball of bread, dried porridge, raisins, and lint. "You can have it if you want. I won't be needing it now." He smiled.

Ida snatched the bizarre lump and ate it in three quick bites. She waited for it to reach her stomach and fill the overpowering void. She soon began to think a little clearer and her dizziness ceased.

"Thanks, Clarence. I'm glad I tripped over your hole."

"Yeah, me too."

"We should get out of here. The Brothers will be out soon, and I don't like the look of that house."

"That's my home."

"It is?" Ida was embarrassed. "It has really nice . . . gutters."

"Thanks."

"Are your parents there?"

"No. My parents are in Gulm, I think. I live with the Master."

"The Master? He lives there?" Ida instinctively began speaking in whispers. "Why didn't you say something earlier?"

"I thought you knew. Everyone knows the Master lives there."

"Was he trying to kill you?"

"No. It's just my turn."

"For what?"

"For the Brothers. They sleep over there." He pointed to an ancient oak tree with an opening at the bottom. "The Master says that as long as the Brothers have children to nourish them, they can live forever."

Ida felt sick. "That's . . . that's horrible. So they were going to eat us?"

"No. Not like this . . ." Clarence began to move his teeth as though he were chewing on a tough piece of beef. He stopped and continued, "The way they eat—it's more like a plant that sucks water out of the dirt."

"So the Brothers are the plants?"

"Precisely!" he said, excited that Ida understood.

But Ida did not feel excited. "What does it feel like?"

"It starts as a tickle in your stomach, and then it feels like ants are stinging your toes, and then your whole body shakes like this . . ." He began to twitch and convulse, with his eyes bulging and his tongue sticking out.

"Okay, okay. I get it." Ida put her hands on his shoulders and forced him to be still. She had felt the pain he'd described at least four times over the past few days.

"Does it make you sick or anything?"

"Not sick, really. But you can't do it too many times, or your brain turns to porridge. And then there's the age thing."

"What age thing?"

Suddenly the oak tree shook and a low growl crept across the field. Ida grabbed Clarence by the neck of his grimy shirt. "We've got to get out of here. Now!"

"Okay," Clarence chirped. "As soon as we have the others."

"Others?"

Clarence gestured at the field, and as Ida focused more, she could see dozens of holes spread over the land. She realized, to her dismay, that each one probably contained a child like herself or Clarence.

"If we're going to Gulm, we have to take them, too," Clarence said.

"Clarence, we don't have time. The Brothers are coming!"

"No. I'd say we have"—he looked over at the rising sun—"at least an hour."

"Just my luck," Ida muttered, but she knew there was a chance that Fargus was in one of these holes. So they began to run around the field, calling down holes, listening for the frightened voices waiting at the bottom.

THIRTY-SIX

Josephine was getting blisters on her hands. It was the reins rubbing her palms. She suddenly remembered her gloves. She reached into her pocket and pulled them out, all wrinkled and scrunched together. It was the first time in her life she was happy to put on a pair of gloves.

She was in love with her horse, Mabel. The mare behaved as if Josephine had been riding her forever. She was sensitive to every turn or change Josephine wanted her to make. Her chestnut hair glistened with the perspiration of their journey and Josephine imagined washing her and brushing out her lovely mane and tail.

Maybe she could take Mabel home with her? After all, Morgan had never said how big the wormhole was.

"You can't take the horse with you!" Ned exclaimed.

Rats, Josephine thought, realizing she must have been talking to herself again. *How embarrassing.*

"I know that," she told Ned.

He was ahead of her, on Thistle. They had been riding for more than an hour now. The forest had impossibly high trees with trunks as wide as grain silos. The sunlight filtered through the leaves in narrow beams that grew wider as they bounced off the earth, and when Josephine looked up into the canopy, she saw butterflies and insects flitting in and out of the light. It felt so quiet, like an enormous church, the trees supporting the sky like wooden pillars.

Josephine knew it was odd, with so much danger and uncertainty lying ahead, but at this moment, she felt quite happy. She dropped her head back and bellowed, "Hello to the sky!" and listened as her voice was slowly swallowed by the enormous space.

Ned's head spun around. "Shh! Are you mental? Do you want the Brothers to hear us?"

"But don't they work for the Master?"

"Yeah."

"And hasn't the Master invited me to dinner?"

"Yeah."

"So?"

"So just shut your gob, will you? Maybe *you're* invited, but I'm *not.*"

Josephine got quiet. He was right. She was being reckless (something she had never been at home).

"Thank you, Ned," she offered in a whisper.

"For what?" he asked.

"For helping me."

"That's what friends do," he answered, turning back around to the path ahead.

"Are we friends?" Josephine asked happily.

"Of course we are. Don't be stupid."

And Josephine grinned from ear to ear, not minding one bit that she had just been called stupid.

THIRTY-SEVEN

Bruce's stomach had started to grumble for lunch. He was deep within the forest and he wished he had thought to bring sandwiches. He also missed his pipe and he had a blister on the back of his right heel. He plopped down on a dead log and took off his shoes.

It was time to consider his situation. He dared not return home today. Or tomorrow, for that matter. Sometimes it took Alma a week to get over her anger. And she had thrown pots at him. She had never done that before. Bruce knew of a nice cave by a stream where he had stayed in the past when Alma had thrown him out. It was not luxurious by any means, but it was a place to sleep.

The thought of sleep made his head droop and he considered a short nap. But just then he heard something in the woods. His eyes bulged.

Someone or *something* was walking toward him.

He wanted to run. But when he jumped up, his legs got intertwined and he fell over. He looked up in terror, waiting for the Brothers to emerge. He could almost smell their earthy aroma, that haunting mixture of fresh-cut grass and rotting compost. The footsteps got louder and Bruce could hear the branches and undergrowth being crushed. He began to crawl away, stifling a shriek. He looked back and saw the branches parting, and he steadied himself against passing out. He began to mutter what he thought would be his last words . . .

. . . when a horse emerged from the thicket. And on the horse's back was a teenage boy.

Bruce exhaled, embarrassed at his own cowardice.

The boy hadn't noticed him yet, but a moment later a second horse came through the trees. This one carried a bushy-haired girl.

"Josephine!" Bruce cried.

Both children saw Bruce and flinched in fear, causing their horses to rear up.

Bruce stood up and stuttered, "You're s-s-safe! I'm so glad. Alma and I have been worried." What blind luck! If he returned home with Josephine in hand, Alma would have to forgive him!

Josephine replied with stony anger, "Worried? You

gave Ida and Fargus to the Master, and you were about to do the same with me."

Bruce was surprised and then shamed. "I—we—you're right. We did. But I—I really was worried about all of you and I'm . . ." He hung his head and mumbled, "I'm glad you're okay."

"Let's go, Josephine," Ned said. "We're in a hurry." He steered his horse past Bruce, one hand resting on his father's hunting knife, but Josephine didn't move. She wasn't finished with Bruce.

"How could you?" she asked. "I thought you were a nice person!"

"I . . . uh . . . Alma said . . ." But he couldn't finish. He knew there was no excuse for what he had done. And he no longer had the energy to try to recapture Josephine.

"Come on," Ned urged again. Josephine kicked Mabel gently, and the horse followed Ned and Thistle. Josephine passed Bruce, disgust in her eyes, and had almost disappeared back into the trees when she stopped and turned around to face him once more. She decided to take a risk. "The bedroom I slept in—whose room was it?"

Bruce was surprised by the question and answered in a whisper, "Her name was Sarah."

"Your daughter?"

He nodded, looking like a child admitting he was afraid of the dark.

"Don't you want to know what happened to Sarah?"

"Of course I do," he mumbled.

"Come with us, then. Ned and I are going to see the Master, to find Fargus and Ida."

Ned whipped around. "You can't trust him! He's the reason your friends are with the Master in the first place!"

Josephine ignored Ned's warning. "Will you help us, Bruce?"

As he stood there, Bruce thought of teaching Ida and Fargus to fish, just as he had done with Sarah so many years ago. Fargus had been unable to flick his wrist and kept getting tangled in the line, and Ida hadn't had the patience to sit and wait for a bite. She'd been ready to jump into the water and grab a trout by hand. They were good kids. Bruce knew that. He had been too determined to please his wife to think for himself.

Bruce stiffened. "You're right, Ned. You have no reason to trust me, but you're not headed in the right direction to get to the Master's estate. At least let me take you there."

"He's old and he's a traitor!" Ned cried. "We don't need him!"

Josephine argued, "We've passed this same dead log three times, Ned. We're lost, and I have to be there by seven!"

"Why does he know the way so well? Because he works for the Master!" Ned barked.

"No," Bruce said. "After he took my daughter, I used to go there. I thought maybe I'd get a glimpse of her, you know? Please, let me help you." Bruce looked up at the sun to get his bearings and then set off toward the Master's estate. Josephine nudged Mabel after him.

"I know the way just fine!" Ned protested.

Bruce and Josephine disappeared farther into the forest. Ned was completely flabbergasted. Bruce looked back and saw Josephine smiling down at him from her horse and Ned and Thistle scrambling to catch up. For the first time in years, Bruce felt as tall as a spruce.

THIRTY-EIGHT

Clarence did most of the climbing in and out of the holes while Ida herded the children together as if she were a sheepdog. She and Clarence now stood on the edge of the field, surrounded by a dozen wide-eyed, dirt-covered children. Ida did not see Fargus among them.

She announced, "All right, all of you, you're safe now, but we have to move fast. The Brothers are about to wake up. Everyone take your neighbor's hand. We're going to move in a line."

"Where are we going?" asked a small girl with orange hair.

"To Gulm."

There was an excited whisper among the group.

"But first, has anyone here seen my friend Fargus? He's a runt about this high, with sandy hair, and he's as talkative as my left shoe."

The children all nodded their heads in unison, although the orange-haired girl asked her neighbor why Ida had a talking shoe. "Where is he?" Ida asked, relieved that he had been seen, but even as she asked the question, she was afraid she knew the miserable answer. The children one by one pointed to the manor.

"Okay. Change of plans. First, we're going to go get Fargus, and then I'll take you to Gulm."

"But what about Mary?" a voice in the middle asked.

"Who's Mary?" Ida asked.

"She's still in her hole. Over there." The boy pointed across the field to an area a mere ten yards from the Brothers' tree. Ida looked at the sky and saw the screaming sun emerging over the hills.

She was annoyed. "Why didn't you say something earlier?" But she looked around at the expectant faces and knew she could not leave anyone behind, however tempting it might be. "Right. Clarence, you come with me. We'll get Mary. The rest of you, wait here."

A boy said, "But they'll see us the second they come out."

Ida looked around and saw a group of tall dead trees near the back of the manor. "I suggest you run as fast as you can to those trees. Climb them and don't make a sound. Don't even breathe."

One child began to stammer in fear, "B-b-but what about . . . ?"

"Just do it. Now!" Ida grabbed Clarence's wrist and began running toward the Brothers' tree. As they drew closer to the entrance to Mary's hole, a deep snort rumbled through the terrain at their feet. Ida looked over her shoulder and saw the sun threatening to douse them in gold. All she could focus on was getting to the hole. She had no idea what she would do once she got there. The ground shook again as a second snarl echoed through the dirt, across the field, and out of the empty holes, and Clarence began to stumble. Ida steadied him and pulled him along behind her. Her nostrils filled with the stench of creatures not made to walk above the earth. The first bold rays of light flickered onto the field. "This is it, Clarence." They had only a few yards left.

"They're coming, Ida."

She looked over to see a black steaming head emerging from the base of the tree. It blinked at the morning air, as if it were entering the world for the first time. And then it suddenly snapped its neck toward them, the smell of young flesh pulling its head around like a leash. Ida leaped across the final few steps and dove into the slim hole. She had neglected to release Clarence's hand and so he toppled in on top of her.

The other children watched in terror from the trees.

They saw Ida and Clarence disappear just as the Brothers rose up. A lanky boy named Kevin was the only one who dared to speak. "They're trapped." Eleven voices told him to shush.

Ida and Clarence had landed with a hard thud at the bottom of the hole. Luckily, Mary was curled into a tight little ball on the far end and had not been hurt. She was surprised to see them, to say the least, and she blinked twice and said, "Ida?"

Ida squinted and recognized Mary Grouse, who had lived at the Institute until only two months ago when Stairway Ruth had sent her to the Master. "Mousy Grouse?" she asked.

"Don't call me that! I hate that!" Mary whimpered.

"You've got bigger problems, Grouse. The Brothers are right outside."

Clarence undid the ropes binding Mary's hands and feet while Ida slowly crawled halfway back up the hole. She listened closely. There was nothing at first, but soon she heard a phlegmy exhale, followed by a wicked growl. The Brothers were almost on top of the hole. She dared not move. The creatures were much too large to climb down, but she had no idea what they were capable of. She muttered to herself, "Out of the frying pan and into the hole."

The children in the trees held their breath as they

watched the Brothers sniff the air and begin to circle, looking for a way down. Kevin whispered to the others, "The Brothers will break their necks for trying to escape. They'll never make it."

A tough girl named Genevieve whispered back, "I'll bet you five puddings they do."

"You're on," Kevin said, although he secretly hoped he would lose the bet.

Genevieve gasped. One of the Brothers had begun to dig at the entrance to the hole, his large claws scooping up the dirt as if it were sand. The other Brother saw him and quickly caught on. He was soon digging next to him.

Ida watched with horror from below as loose dirt rained down on them. A large wet patch landed on Clarence. "Ida, what is this?" He held up the slime for Ida to inspect.

She looked at it and grimaced. "That would be Brother snot."

Clarence shrieked and wiped his hand on the dirt wall. Mary giggled, but as Ida watched the claws tearing away above her, she knew that there was *nothing* to laugh about.

THIRTY-NINE

Ned was irritated. They were moving at a painfully slow pace. Bruce held Mabel's reins and led her and Josephine through the trees while Ned followed. What was the point of horses if one person had to walk? He grumbled and ground his teeth a bit, but neither Bruce nor Josephine noticed. They were engrossed in their own conversation.

"Sarah was tall for her age, which she hated," Bruce said, "but I knew she was going to be a real beauty. Just like her mother."

Josephine must have looked surprised, because Bruce said, "It's hard to see now, but Alma was quite the looker in her day."

Ned snorted. He'd known Alma Jarvis his whole life, and she was nothing but a wrinkled shrew. Then Josephine turned to him and said, "The Master's house is just ahead." Ned's heart quickened. He had been so focused on their slow pace that he had almost forgotten their destination. He felt for his father's knife and patted it for reassurance.

The forest had become strangely quiet. No birds were singing, and he felt that even the breeze had decided it could go no farther. The vegetation became sparser and sparser as they continued, and soon there were only dead trees and dirt, as if the Master's presence had sucked the life out of everything nearby. Ned could hardly believe they were still in Gulm.

Up ahead, Bruce had stopped walking, and he helped Josephine dismount Mabel, telling her to crouch behind a dead tree. Next he went to help Ned off Thistle, but Ned leaped off nimbly before Bruce reached him.

Ned was sorry to say good-bye to his noble steed, and he stroked the stallion's mane and said, "Time to go home, Thistle."

"Thistle?" Bruce laughed.

"Shut up!" Ned snapped. "It's a good name!" He slapped the horse on the rear end and Thistle immediately trotted toward home, with Mabel close on his heels.

Ned turned to see Bruce pointing at something up ahead—the Master's manor. A quiver ran down his spine. This was where it had happened: the destruction of his father's family, the disappearance of his aunt, Lucy, and the fight that had cost Morgan the use of one of his legs.

Bruce spoke in a low whisper. "Maybe we should wait until dark, to make sure the Brothers aren't around."

But Josephine shook her head. "The invitation said quite clearly that I was expected at seven o'clock."

"She's right," Ned agreed. "We have to risk it."

"How will you get in?" Josephine asked, staring at the huge iron door and moat.

"You approach the front door and announce yourself, which will cause a diversion so I can sneak around the side."

"And what should she do once she's in there?" Bruce wondered.

"I don't know," Ned said. "Make small talk, have tea, talk about her cousins. Whatever it is that relatives do when they drop in."

"And you think the Master will just let her leave when the dinner is over, maybe walk her to the door with a pot of jam?" Bruce asked in a voice dripping with sarcasm.

Ned told Josephine, "You just have to keep him busy long enough for me to find Ida and Fargus."

"How will I know if you've had enough time?"

"Eat dinner," Ned said. "Talk about his nice house or

moat or whatever, and then you get out!" His voice soft-
ened. "Don't stay any longer than you have to, okay?"

"But what if you—"

"He's right," Bruce added. "No matter what Ned and I
find, you have to leave there as soon as you can."

Ned swung around. "What!? You aren't coming with
me!" He couldn't imagine this oaf trying to swim, let
alone shimmy up a wall.

"I've come this far. I want to help. . . ."

Ned sighed. "You can be my lookout, but that's it. I'm
not dragging any tired old bones into the manor. You'll
only slow me down."

Bruce fought the urge to admonish the boy for being
so rude. He knew it would take time for Ned to trust
him. He simply nodded his head in agreement.

"Where will I meet you?" Josephine asked.

"Back here at this dead tree. If I'm not here by midnight with Ida and Fargus, then you have to go to
the Institute. Bruce, can you lead her to the Higgins
Institute?"

"Over in the plains?"

Ned nodded.

"Yeah, I suppose I could find that," Bruce answered,
happy to be needed.

Josephine said to Ned, "But you'll be here. I know
you will." She walked over and gave Ned a hug, so star-

tling him that he nearly fell over. She then stood on tip-toe and gave Bruce a hug too. "I'd better get going."

They both wished her luck and forced smiles, but Josephine could see the worry in their eyes.

She turned from them and walked toward the manor, her blood running furiously through her veins. *What have I got myself into?* She crossed the field and practiced her greeting under her breath. "Hello, my name is Josephine Russing. . . . This food is just delightful. . . . Mama sends her love from the South." Surely he would know she was full of lard.

And would the Master be able to explain why he and her father shared the same name? Josephine knew there was part of her that was afraid to know the answer.

She looked down and saw she was still wearing her shiny gloves. She stuck them back into her pocket and then tried to smooth her blue dress. Ever since Ned had thrown her into the spring, it had been in desperate need of a wash. It was wrinkled and sad looking. And after that horseback ride, she knew her hair must look a fright. She patted down her tangled tresses and tried to retie her headband. Unfortunately, there was not much more she could do.

She approached the manor and suddenly the draw-bridge began to lower, as if it had known the precise moment she would be arriving.

As Josephine grew closer, she could make out a crouching figure in an orange hat who seemed to be waiting for her. He was old and looked as if he was in pain. Nevertheless, he offered her a warm smile, and as she crossed the drawbridge, he put an arm around her shoulder.

"Welcome, miss. We've been expecting you."

"Yes. My name is—"

"Miss Josephine Russing. We know, dear. Perhaps a nice cup of tea?"

Josephine was terribly confused. This man seemed so gentle. "Are you the Master?"

The elderly man let out a hoot of amusement. "Gracious no, miss. I'm Mr. Seaworthy. I am here to make sure you are comfortable. Won't you come in?" He stepped back and motioned her inside. Josephine tentatively walked forward, and although she was tempted to look back toward the dead tree, she was careful not to give Bruce and Ned away.

Mr. Seaworthy led her into a small courtyard filled with marble statues of men of enormous height and strength. Curiously, the heads were missing from nearly all of them, and some arms and legs had gone missing from others. Mr. Seaworthy caught her perplexed look. "The Master likes to use these for sword practice when he is feeling a bit . . . youthful." He unbolted one of several doors opening onto the courtyard and waved Josephine inside.

She found a study of sorts, with a warm fire in the corner and overstuffed chairs made of fine leather. There was a substantial library, and against one wall there were many clocks of various shapes and sizes, although none of them appeared to be working. On a high shelf, looking lost and maudlin, were the marble heads of the statues outside.

"Monstrous," Josephine mumbled.

"Do you think so?" A small voice startled her. She turned to see a boy, a few years younger than herself, dressed in some sort of maritime uniform. Had Morgan said anything about the Master having a family?

"Excuse me, I didn't hear you enter. My name is Josephine."

"Yes, I know."

"I believe I'm here to see your father."

"That would be difficult. He's been dead for fifty years." He walked over to the fireplace and took a crystal decanter from the mantel. "May I offer you a brandy?"

Brandy? This boy was no more than ten! "No, thank you."

"Suit yourself. Please sit down."

Josephine was completely befuddled. This boy spoke with authority but looked as if he were playing dress-up.

She tried to hide her discomfort. "You know my name, but I'm afraid I don't know yours."

The boy laughed. "You are wildly polite, aren't you? My name is Leopold Reginald Russing, but you can call me Master."

Josephine had to steady herself against a chair. This was the same evil boy whom Morgan had told her about—the one that shared her father's name—and he hadn't aged a day in twenty years. She had no idea how it was possible. It felt like madness, and yet a tiny relieved voice in the back of her head was saying, "At least it's not my father."

She attempted to collect herself and said casually, "So you're also a Russing? I *do* think it is great fun to have discovered a new relative, don't you?" She tried smiling.

The boy grinned back, enjoying her distress. "I thought everyone was dead!" he replied. "And yet here you are. . . ." His eyes turned dark. "And how is that, Josephine? How did you come to be in Gulm?"

"I d-don't know," she stammered.

"Not good enough, I'm afraid. Try again."

"I don't know, really."

"I'm going to tell you a little story over dinner, and we'll see if it helps to jog your memory."

Josephine stared at the boy and now saw nothing but malice in his plastic grin.

FORTY

Ned and Bruce quietly approached the west side of the manor. They had watched the drawbridge lower to welcome Josephine, and as soon as it had closed again, they'd started running across the field. Ned concentrated on stepping lightly, painfully aware of how exposed they were in the daylight. There was a small cluster of trees next to the rear of the manor that would provide some cover, and Ned was about twenty yards away when a small shoe hit him square in the face.

Ned yelped in pain and Bruce froze in his tracks. Soon another shoe came flying from the trees and caught Bruce in the shin. Next a sandal grazed Ned's ear.

Bruce said, "Either that tree likes footwear, or someone's hiding up there."

Ned took another step forward and saw a second

sandal hurtling toward him. He ducked just in time and took another two steps. "Hello? Who's up there?"

"No one!" came a voice from above.

"Oh great, Francis. *Now* they'll go away."

"Shush," said several others.

"But Kevin threw my sandals!"

"It's children!" Bruce exclaimed.

"Children with a mean right hook," said Ned, as he rubbed his chin. "Strange place to play, if you ask me." He spoke into the tops of the trees. "My name's Ned. And this is Bruce."

Bruce attempted a weak smile. "We don't want to hurt you."

"PROVE IT," one of the children yelled.

"Uh, well, we know that the Master lives here, and we want to rescue some children we think are inside."

Kevin dropped out of the tree and faced them, armed with a yellow boot. "*We* live inside. Who are you looking for?"

Bruce was taken aback to hear that the Master still had many kidnapped children. He hadn't raided the town in years. Where had he gotten them all?

Ned told Kevin, "Well, we want to help a boy and girl named Fargus and Ida, but we're prepared to help all of you, if you want."

"Why?" Kevin asked, suspicious.

Bruce stepped forward. "My daughter, Sarah, was taken from me a long time ago. And a day hasn't gone by that I don't think about her. We just want to help those two children get home."

There were whispers in the tree and an air of excitement. A girl dropped down and landed by Kevin.

Bruce wasn't entirely sure he was awake, because for a moment he thought the girl standing in front of him was his young daughter, Sarah.

She said, "Poppa?"

Bruce squinted at the girl and then at Ned and then back at the girl.

She approached him with arms wide. "It's Sarah!"

Bruce took a step backward, unable to believe his eyes. "It's nice to meet you," he said, "but you can't be . . . My Sarah was taken more than twenty years ago . . . and you're only . . ." This girl had the same brown hair and green eyes of his daughter, but she looked no older than ten. Sarah smiled and Bruce's eyes filled with tears. "I don't know what kind of joke you're playing, but it's . . . it's very cruel."

"It's no joke." She took a few steps closer to him. "My name is Sarah Jarvis. I was born on the fifteenth of June. My favorite color is purple. My mother is Alma, and when I was three, I ran into the kitchen table and nearly blinded myself. You can still see the scar."

Bruce approached her cautiously and looked at her

face. Underneath her right eye was a small pink dot. Sarah whispered, "And last summer I turned twenty-nine."

Bruce tried to process the information, his tall frame swaying a bit with the confusion. He took several large gulps of air and then reached his hand out to touch the tiny scar. He felt that she was real, that her scar was made of flesh, and then he grabbed her and hugged her as if he'd never felt a real flesh-and-blood person before in his life.

"I'm sorry. I'm so sorry, Sarah. I should have come sooner. I should have found you. . . ." Tears ran down his cheeks and landed in her hair.

"It's okay. It's going to be fine." She patted his back. "How's Mother?"

Ned was gobsmacked. "What's going on around here? How can that *girl* be twenty-nine?"

"We'd love to explain, but we still have a major problem here," said Kevin.

"What is it?" Bruce asked.

Kevin pointed across the field. Ned looked, and in the far distance he could just make out the outline of the Brothers.

"They've been there all day. They've trapped three of us inside. Clarence, Mary, and your friend Ida."

"Ida rescued us from the feeding holes," one of the children yelled down from a branch. "We have to help her."

"Feeding holes?" Ned asked.

Bruce seemed to remember where he was, and without releasing his grip on Sarah, he said, "Can't we just wait until nightfall, when the Brothers disappear?"

"They'll reach the bottom by then," Kevin explained, and added ominously, "And all three of them will be goners."

"All right," Ned said. "Then we need a plan."

"How many children are left in the manor?" Bruce asked Sarah.

The children conversed among themselves for a moment. Sarah said, "Probably fifty or more."

Bruce surveyed the field. "Ned, you go on to the house. These children and I will take care of the Brothers."

"What?" Ned and Sarah asked simultaneously.

"I know these woods better than anyone. And if you think I'm taking Sarah back into that manor, you're crazy. I'm going to get the children out of that hole and then I am going to take all of these boys and girls home to their families."

"Watch who you call boy," Kevin said. "I happen to be thirty-one."

"Sorry about that, young man." He turned back to Ned. "Get going. We've already wasted too much time."

"Okay. I'll go get the others. Take these children— I mean, people—back to town and I'll contact you as soon as I can." He looked at Sarah, her young face hiding wizened eyes. "Nice to meet you, Sarah. I've heard a lot about you."

"It's nice to meet you, too. I have no idea who you are."

"This is Ned the sweeper's son," Bruce offered. "See you soon, Ned."

"See you soon. And . . . uh . . . thanks, Bruce." Ned then sprinted toward the western wall of the building.

Bruce told the children to come out of the trees. One by one, they plopped down like overripe apples, and Bruce inspected his new team. He felt young for the first time in twenty years. "Okay, troops. Who here has ever played tag?"

FORTY-ONE

The Master swirled his brandy around a large snifter and took a long gulp. He swallowed, belched loudly, and stood up. He and Josephine had just finished a mountain of food. Josephine was stuffed to the gills and sat uncomfortably in a massive wooden chair as she waited for the Master to continue his story. He was telling her about his childhood.

"My mother was an exquisite beauty, but she was raised in dung. Her family was absolutely destitute. My grandparents were both plain as old toast, and they never understood how they'd produced such magnificence. In fact, they were so mystified by her existence that they barely touched her, as if she were made of rice paper and might just blow away." The Master took another swig of brandy and walked to the fireplace.

"Many of the local men sought her hand. But she

was determined to wait for"—he paused disdainfully—
"true love." He rolled his eyes and continued. "One day,
my father appeared out of nowhere. My mother's first
impression of him was that he was a short, boring,
pimply snob. It turned out she was wrong about one
thing: He wasn't that short. He offered her parents an
exorbitant amount of money for her hand, and he was
allowed to take her that very day to his family's estate in
Drubshire. She never forgave him. He was a weak man
and he had made the ghastly mistake of loving her.

"When I was four, my father disappeared. Mummy
always said it was a hunting accident, but I caught the
servants rolling their eyes. Once he was gone, she was
determined to find the true love that had eluded her.
She stopped eating, concerned that childbirth had made
her fat."

He walked back to the table and pinched off a juicy
grape, then rolled it between his fingers. "She would
bother the servants all day long with elaborate details
about supper—which spices and sauces should be used,
which goose should be slaughtered, how many elaborate pastries should be baked—and then she wouldn't
eat one bite. I used to worry that the cook would have
hurt feelings, so I would eat twice my fill."

He popped the grape into his mouth. "I became quite
the little butterball, which only served to antagonize my

mother more. As she continued to fast, the flesh began to hang off her bones, and her face became so tight that one could see the blood moving under her skin. Her hips and bosom disappeared and she took to wearing large embroidered dresses of heavy fabrics. I once heard the maid say that when Mummy walked down the stairway, she looked like a teeny skull perched upon some drapes."

The Master laughed nastily, but Josephine didn't think it was funny at all. "Her gaunt fingers allowed her rings to fall off without her noticing," he continued. "The servants gathered them up like candy. I imagine it's how a few of them retired.

"Many suitors arrived. Mummy's beauty had been legendary and now her fortune was too. I would sit at the dinner table across from the poor chap of the moment, who was inevitably trying not to stare at my mother's bulging eyes and cheekbones. She would attempt to be charming but would never smile. The suitor was always thrown by her stony expression as she explained what a delightful time she was having. What he never knew was that she didn't smile because lack of nutrition had rotted her teeth.

"As one by one they stopped paying her visits, she became more miserable and venomous. She decided that I was the one turning them away and that they were sickened by a woman who was already a mother. She forbade me to sit at the dinner table. I was not allowed outside or anywhere strangers might spot me. She had the servants construct a 'playroom' down in the cellar. It smelled of onions and dead rats, and I was ordered to stay there during the daytime."

Josephine thought this was perhaps the worst thing she'd ever heard. Her father was not an affectionate man, but he'd never been cruel or hateful toward her. She felt herself softening toward the Master and thought that maybe she understood why he was so mean. "That's awful," she said.

"Don't interrupt," he told her. "One winter, before my ninth birthday, she became infatuated with a new man, Count Luther Von Wottleton. He visited her several times and she managed to keep me hidden. The servants knew better than to mention her son, having seen the welts on past offenders. Mummy was quite taken with this man, and from my cellar window I would watch them walk in the gardens. He would do most of the talking, and she giggled and sometimes forgot to cover her mouth with her hand. I had never seen her happier. She even brought me sweets and took me on a long walk when the count was out of town." A small smile crept onto the Master's face at the memory and Josephine found herself smiling too, relieved that the Master may have had at least a tiny moment of joy in his childhood.

"But it didn't last long. The count didn't come back. At first Mummy told the servants that his business was keeping him away. But as several more weeks passed, she became quiet and depressed. Finally, word reached her that the count had married his cousin. And the fatal blow came when Mummy heard that the girl was only nineteen. She flew into a rage and broke all the heirlooms in the house.

"Then she disappeared. She vanished into the night wearing plain clothes and a cloak. None of us knew what to do. The servants ran the house as usual, anticipating her eventual return, and I spent my time with them in the kitchen. After a few weeks, things relaxed and we started to do as we pleased. We all ate around the dining room table and one night we even had a food fight. It was the happiest time I'd ever known. An older couple named Mr. and Mrs. Baggs, who tended the gardens, asked if I wanted to come and live with them. I said yes immediately. And at that one moment, I thought at last I was going to have a normal childhood, with friends."

Josephine thought about Bruce and Alma Jarvis and how she had briefly thought she could have a normal childhood living with them. And once again her heart felt the sting of their betrayal.

"And then Mummy came back. She returned in the middle of winter, just as the clock struck midnight. But she wasn't alone. The Brothers walked close behind her. Some of the servants fled in terror, including the Baggses, who begged me to go with them. But I couldn't. I was frozen. She was my mother.

"She looked triumphant, grinning from ear to ear as she showed me her black hole of a mouth. 'I've done it, Leopold! I've found the fountain of youth!' She swung me around maniacally. I thought she'd completely lost her mind. 'I was given these marvelous creatures,' she said, 'and tonight Mummy is going to bury herself in the ground next to them and they are going to suck all of Mummy's years away, and I will *never* grow old! *Never*, Leopold!'

"She explained how she'd met a man one cold night on the road, who seemed to appear out of nowhere. He claimed to have traveled to the Dark World, where he stole the Brothers from their mother while they were still harmless pups."

Josephine flinched. "That's horrible. Why should they want to obey anyone who did that to them?"

The Master pulled a strange-looking stone from his pocket. It was multicolored like an opal, yet it was translucent and seemed to glow from the inside. He explained, "It's lava rock from the Dark World. And the Brothers are tied to it like an umbilical cord." He added smugly, "Don't get any ideas, Josephine. They will always do exactly as I command." He made a fist around the stone.

"Where was I when you so rudely interrupted? Oh yes, Mummy's return. That night, we all watched as the Brothers dug their way into a deep pit and Mummy piled dirt on top of them. She then had a servant dig a long narrow hole for herself. She was wearing her finest silks and gold, and, looking as happy as I'd ever seen her, she lowered herself into the dank soil. We waited to see what would happen. It didn't take long. Mummy began screaming in agony, crying out for help. The servants just stood there, but I couldn't stand it. I rushed to the hole to see Mummy convulsing, and pustules were forming on her flesh. It was foul. I jumped into the hole and gathered her in my arms. Her skin was turning dry and her hair so brittle that it fell off in strands into my lap. And then do you know what she said to me?"

Josephine shook her head, not wanting to know.

"She smiled at me and said, 'I should have known you were the only one pathetic enough to love me.' And then she disintegrated, simply turned to dust in my arms, and the only thing left was the lava stone.

"And then my real pain began. The Brothers had finished with Mummy and now it was my turn. Their draining power reached deep within me and I convulsed helplessly, waiting for the pustules, the swelling, and my eventual death, but it didn't come. The pain ended and I was able to climb back out of the hole. It was years later before I understood why. The man who sold the Brothers to my mother had neglected to tell her that as long as the creatures were in our world, they could only properly feed off children. For an adult to be buried with them was certain death. But he was correct about one thing. If a child feels the pain of a Brother feeding, he will *never* grow old, even if he desperately wants to."

A word came to Josephine, something from one of her books. *"Succulents,"* she uttered without thinking.

"Excuse me?" said the Master.

"Uh . . . the Brothers, they're *succulents*. Like cacti? They don't eat, really; they suck nutrients out of the soil around them." She pictured the dead and barren wasteland outside the manor and knew she was right.

He smiled an evil, bitter grin. "You're not altogether stupid for your age. It took me quite a while to figure that out. It seems that something in the soil of the Dark World gives the Brothers all they need, but here in our world, they need a little—how shall I say it—supplement?"

"The lost children of Gulm," she gasped. "You didn't

sell them at all. You've just been feeding them to the Brothers."

The Master did a little bow, as if Josephine had paid him an enormous compliment.

"How long can they survive it?" she asked, horrified.

"Oh, years and years. It's wonderful, actually. A very efficient fueling system."

"But those poor children . . . cooped up here with you . . . You've stolen their lives!"

"Enough!" he spat, slamming his fist onto the table, rattling the dishes and candlesticks. "I didn't tell you this story to elicit a lecture. I told you this story so that you would understand how it is that you can help me."

"I'm sorry, I still don't see . . ."

The Master banged his fist down on the table again, causing the dinner plates and glasses to shake. "Stop lying to me! Can't you see? I need more! Two just isn't enough. I can rule this pathetic little town with two, but that's nothing! If I had an army of Brothers . . . now, that would be something. I would be unstoppable. I could rule the world!"

He walked toward her ominously. "But I have to know where to go, Josephine. I need to know where the entrance is to your world. And I'm afraid if you don't tell me, I will have to get very unpleasant." She thought of the Brothers, their beady yellow eyes and razor-sharp claws, and knew she didn't want to learn what he meant by "unpleasant."

"Even if I could explain how to travel from your world to mine, which I can't, you wouldn't find any Brothers there. I promise—I've never seen any."

"Josephine, you are very adorable *and* very naive. I don't need the location of your world, I need the location of the door. Once I have the door, I can go wherever I please, to any other world or time, and bring back whatever I need. Now, once more, how did you find the door? I want every detail."

"I . . . uh . . . was in my shed, and I was looking for my shovel when I tripped over a spade, and when I woke up, I was here." Josephine felt it was vital that she not mention Fargus. She didn't want the Master knowing that Fargus had found the door too.

"You just tripped? That's it? Well, how lucky you must be. Many men have wasted their whole lives looking for a way into other worlds, and yet you happened to fall into it. Somehow I find that hard to believe. I think I have something that might change your story." He walked to the wall and pulled a cord. Mr. Seaworthy appeared.

"Bring him in." Mr. Seaworthy left and returned with Fargus close behind.

"Fargus!" Josephine cried, before she had time

to think. Fargus looked at her in surprise, and for a moment it seemed as though he might run toward her. But he restrained himself and walked toward the Master and bowed.

Josephine could see that Fargus's left hand had been bandaged and he appeared to be in some pain.

The Master put his hand on Fargus's shoulder and said gleefully, "Young Fargus here has decided to become my aide and confidant."

Josephine was shocked. "You're lying. He would never work for you."

"Oh but he does. And together, you two are going to tell me the truth about the door."

FORTY-TWO

Ned crept toward the moat. He had found what he considered to be the best chance of entering the manor: a small window on the first story. The exterior walls were made of a thick stone that would make for good footholds. He just needed to swim across the moat and begin climbing.

There was only one problem. The moat smelled terrible, like rotten eggs, and Ned had to wonder if maybe the Master used it for his sewage. And the water was inky black, concealing the depth of the moat and what creatures may lurk within. What if there were dangerous fish or poisonous snakes? After all, what good was a moat that was just water?

Finally, he realized he was wasting precious time and that he was being a big sally. He held his breath and dove in.

FORTY-THREE

Fargus had been completely aghast to see Josephine standing in the dining hall, and he could see that Josephine was appalled to see him bowing to the Master. She looked frightened but furious, like a wildcat with its hair on end. She spoke through clenched teeth. "I'm going to explain for the last time that I found the door by accident. If I knew how to find it and return home, believe me, I would have long ago. But Fargus doesn't know anything. He can't even speak."

"Hello, Josephine," Fargus said.

Josephine stared at him in shock. "Fargus? You can talk!"

"Yes, it's amazing what the right guidance can do," the Master snarled.

"The Master says that for every sentence I utter, he

will spare Ida for another day." He looked at the Master. "And that one just made it twenty-three days."

"Ah, language and math in one lesson. Isn't it genius?" asked the Master. Josephine was too shocked to respond. "Now, we have the lovely lady from 'abroad' and the once silent boy now full of jabber. I think we are quite ready to proceed with our conversation. And by the way, every time you lie to me or say you don't know the answer to my questions, you take one day of life *away* from Ida."

Josephine knew she had no choice but to tell the Master everything she knew.

"Leave Josephine alone, Master," Fargus said. "She doesn't know about the door. I found it."

The Master smirked. "You've been holding out on me. Please continue."

"I was in the Institute, playing hide-and-seek with Ida. I decided to hide in the cellar, behind the woodpile. I knew she would never look there because one time we found a spider there, and Ida hates spiders. This other time there was a spider in the wash basin and—"

"Don't make me regret helping you speak. Please stay focused," the Master growled.

"Sorry. Anyway, I was crouched inside like this." Fargus demonstrated his hiding position. "And when I heard Ida coming, I tried to bury myself even more.

That's when the wall moved and I fell like this." He then flayed his hands around as if he were falling from a great height. "Next thing I knew, I was lying on the ground. At first I thought I was still in the Institute, in a hidden room, maybe. There were all sorts of weird tools and things. And then a door opened, and I thought it was Ida so I was real quiet because I wanted to win the game. But it wasn't Ida. It was a girl—I mean, it was her, Josephine. After she left, I waited and then followed her out of the shed because I wanted to see where I was. There was this big white house with lots of green trees, just like the kind I want to live in one day. I was so excited and I wanted to show Ida the house. So I went back into the shed and looked for the door back to the cellar. But there wasn't a door, just a wall. And I got real scared because I thought I was lost, and I started to hit the wall and it moved, or I fell through it—I'm not sure which. And I fell back into the Institute."

"Remarkable!" said the Master. "So you had no special amulet or instrument?"

"No." Fargus thought for a moment. "But I did have some raisins in my pocket."

The Master clapped his hands in glee. "Who knew it would be so simple? All these years I've been trying to discover some great mathematical formula, when all

I needed to do was push on a wall! What do you think, Seaworthy?"

Mr. Seaworthy had propped himself against a leather chair. "Well done, sir. You are brilliant—as usual."

The Master was giddy with excitement. "And that was the only time you went through the door?"

"No. I waited a few days to try again. Ida didn't believe me the first time. So this time I had my suitcase so that I could bring something back from the house. And I went back to the cellar, got behind the woodpile, and curled into a tiny ball, but nothing happened. So I tried again the next day, and the day after that. Each time I tried a different spot behind the woodpile. Until finally, a light flashed and I fell again like this." He once more began to demonstrate falling, but the Master put his hand on the boy's shoulder.

"Yes, we've been through that. Continue."

"And then I met Josephine, and I ate oatmeal with sugar, and she let me sleep in her squashy bed." Josephine couldn't help smiling. It was so good to hear his voice, and it wasn't timid or afraid. It was the voice of a healthy boy.

"But then I missed my friend Ida and I wanted her to see Josephine, so I left."

"Incredible!" the Master said. "So you transported yourself through—"

Just then there was a knock on the door and one of the servants entered.

"I told you not to disturb me!" the Master yelled.

"Yes, sir," the poor man said with down-turned eyes. "It's just that . . . there is an intruder in the house, sir, and he has just breached the western hall."

The Master nodded at him and then gave Josephine a knowing wink. "Your friend the sweeper's son, I suppose?"

Josephine felt as if she had been knocked down a flight of stairs. He knew about Ned! This whole thing had been nothing but a trap.

FORTY-FOUR

Ned stood facing an enormous silver door with no doorknob. Two more just like it were to his left and to his right. As a matter of fact, the entire house seemed to be made up of nothing but silver doors. He wasn't being as quiet as he wanted. He was soaking wet and his shoes squeaked with every step he took. He had been so afraid of nasty creatures in the moat, but it seemed the only real danger after all was the stink. Ned positively reeked. If his *noise* didn't set off any alarms, then certainly his *odor* would.

He had never seen a building like this one. Every hallway seemed to turn back on itself and lead him back to where he started. The walls and ceilings were opalescent, and despite no obvious light source, the space was almost blindingly bright.

No one door looked more safe or dangerous than the

next, so finally he just picked one at random, leaned against it, knocked, and said, "Hello?" After a few moments, a voice came back from the other side.

"Who's there?" It sounded like a young girl.

"I'm Ned, and I'm looking for some children."

"We're children."

"Oh, great!" He couldn't believe his luck. "Do you know how to open this door?"

"Yes. There is a switch on the opposite wall."

Ned saw nothing on the opposite wall but a smooth surface. But as he looked harder, he could see that there was a patch of the wall that seemed less smooth. He touched it, and the door opened behind him. He turned to find a girl with bug eyes and dirty hair standing before him, surprised.

"Who are you?" she asked.

"I'm Ned and I have no time to explain. If you want to get out of here and get back to your families, then you have to leave with me right now."

"You smell."

"I know. But I'm still a good person. We have to hurry." Behind the girl, he saw ten other children looking at him excitedly. "Let's go," he told them. "We have to get everybody else." The children ran out of the room and joined him in the hallway.

"Open all of these doors and make sure you get

everyone out. You go left and I'll go right. Meet back here in five minutes."

The children did as they were told as Ned continued to open the silver doors. He found small groups of drained, bored children behind each one. Each child looked as though he or she had been stuck in a suffocating classroom and forced to take an excruciating and interminable math exam.

As he cleared the last room, some of the children refused to leave. He marched inside. "What's the problem?" he demanded.

"We don't want to leave our friend."

Ned looked down and saw a girl sitting with her knees hugged to her chest. She was rocking slightly and muttering her ABCs. And although she was pale and thin, Ned recognized her immediately as his aunt, Lucy.

"Lucy?" He knelt down. "Lucy . . . you're alive!"

But she did not respond. She kept muttering letters to herself. "M . . . N . . . O . . . P . . ."

"My name is Ned and I'm your brother's son. I've come to help you!" He looked up at the other children helplessly. "What's wrong with her?"

A boy replied, "She went into the holes again last week, and when she came back, she was like this. Sometimes that happens if you don't eat enough the night before."

Ned wanted to cry. Last week! She had been okay until *last* week. He looked back down at his vacant aunt. "Come on, Lucy. We have to get you out of this place." He bent down and picked her up. She weighed less than air. She didn't protest but continued to stare off into nothingness. He ran out of the room holding her, the other children following behind. He headed for the first door, where the others were waiting. By the time he arrived, he saw before him a group of nearly seventy children.

"Okay, listen, everyone. There are a lot of us. I have to lower you out the window one at a time, and then you have to climb down the wall and swim across the moat. Can everyone here do that?"

The children nodded, feeling that they could fly if Ned needed them to.

"Oh," he added, "be sure to hold your noses."

FORTY-FIVE

The Brothers had almost dug to the bottom of the hole. They could smell the three humans, and they grunted and snorted as they clawed at roots and mud.

Down below, Mary, Clarence, and Ida clung to one another as the hole began to crumble around them. Ida coughed as the dirt and dust filled her lungs, and she told Mary to keep her head down. Ida had been in bad situations before, but nothing like this. She could hear the watery snorting of the Brothers and could smell their acrid bodies. She had no ideas, no plan for an escape. They were trapped, and that was it.

She was so frustrated and exhausted and sick of being in a dark hole that she suddenly started screaming a litany of insults at the Brothers.

"Leave us alone, you disgusting, mouthless, snot-nosed, bum-faced freaks! You smell like a pig's backside!"

The other two children stared at her in shock. Ida shrugged, but the truth was, it had made her feel better and less afraid.

Suddenly the Brothers stopped digging, and the snorting and panting stopped. Ida looked at Mary and Clarence. What was happening? Surely they couldn't have understood what she'd said?

What Ida couldn't have known was that up above ground, the Brothers had heard a high-pitched shout from across the field. They had stopped digging to see what it was. And oddly, a child had slowly risen up out of one of the holes and made peeping noises at them.

One of the Brothers went to check it out. But as the creature got closer, the child suddenly disappeared. The Brother turned back toward the hole, but then it heard the chirping again. It turned and saw the same child, slowly rising out of the ground and then disappearing. The Brother stood on its hind feet and walked toward where the boy had been. Then it heard a clatter coming from behind. It turned to see a different child seemingly levitating above the ground. The child, Kevin, was making faces and rude noises at the Brother, which was infuriating to the creature.

Kevin saw the Brother running toward him and

waited as long as he could manage before he yelled, "Now!" The two children he was standing on dropped back down into their hole, hiding all three of them. They heard the Brother grunt in frustration. Kevin looked at his friends and smiled.

Bruce stood tall in a different hole, with Sarah standing on his shoulders. "Do you see them?" he asked her.

"One of them was going after Kevin."

"Good. We want them away from Ida's hole. Now, don't wait too long, honey. As soon as one heads this way, you give me the signal."

"I know. I will." She was shaking with anticipation. Suddenly the other Brother stood up on its hind feet and sprinted straight for Sarah. She felt her muscles suddenly solidify.

"What is it, Sarah? Are they coming?" Bruce asked, annoyed he could see nothing from the bottom of the hole.

The Brother was about to reach her, its claws stretched out in front of it to take off her head, when Bruce heard Sarah squeak in fright and he immediately dropped to his knees. The Brother's paw swiped at the empty air and it landed with a thud on the other side of the hole, confused.

Sarah had toppled in on Bruce and she looked at him apologetically. "Sorry. He came at me so fast . . ."

"It's okay." He hugged her. "But my heart won't survive you doing it twice."

By this point the Brothers were running in circles from hole to hole, always *just* missing the child that was tormenting them. The children continued to bait them, standing on one another's shoulders and always ducking back into their holes as soon as one of the Brothers got near. At last the creatures began panting and their running became labored.

When Bruce felt the Brothers were tired enough, he snuck out of his hole and crept to the edge of the forest. Sarah reluctantly let him go, frightened of losing him again.

At the same moment, the Brothers were heading for Kevin, and Bruce called out to them from across the field. "Hey! Your mother's a snaggletooth and your father smells of scat and onions!"

The Brothers swung their heads simultaneously and saw Bruce, out of the holes and vulnerable. Bruce waved his arms and wiggled his rear at them, and they headed straight for him. They were trying to sprint, but all they could manage now was a strenuous jog. Before they could reach him, Bruce disappeared into the forest, and they angrily followed him.

And then there was an eerie silence.

Ida, Clarence, and Mary peeked out of their hole

and saw that the Brothers were gone. Ida crawled out, relieved to be done with the claustrophobic space. Being in a hole alone had been bad enough, but with two other people! She and Clarence helped Mary up, and they joined the other children, who were climbing out of their own holes and congregating in the middle of the field.

Kevin told Ida that Bruce wanted them to climb back into the tall trees next to the manor until nightfall, when the Brothers would go to sleep. Then Bruce would return to lead them into Gulm.

So the whole group headed back toward the manor and the trees.

Kevin nudged Ida and said, "We really saved your stump back there."

"The only reason they left us alone was because I yelled at them," Ida said with pride.

Kevin smiled. "Yeah. Sure." He had lost the bet with Genevieve and owed her five puddings, but he didn't mind.

Soon the trees were once more full of children. Ida helped Mary climb up and then started to walk away.

Mary balked. "Where are you going?"

"To the house," Ida announced. "To find Fargus. I'll be back."

"Wait!" Mary squeaked.

"What?" said Ida, growing impatient.

Mary began to tear up. "I left Betsy in the hole."

"Who's Betsy?" Ida asked in alarm.

"It's her doll," one of the other children chimed in.

"Oh. Her doll." Ida looked Mary square in the face and replied, "Kid, tough turkey." And with that Ida turned and walked alone toward the manor.

FORTY-SIX

Ned had already lowered ten children out the window and into the water, but he could see that it was going to get very complicated. Some of the children couldn't swim and some were just frightened. Ned tried to locate the strong swimmers to look after the others. It was challenging to treat these young people as the adults they were. His instinct was to order them around like babies. He tried to move as fast as he could, but they had already taken twice as long as he wanted, and they were making enough noise to wake the dead. He nervously looked back at Lucy huddled against the wall, seemingly oblivious to the activity around her. He would carry her down himself.

There was a scream from below. Ned ran to the window and looked down at the moat, expecting to see a drowned child. Instead he saw a boy treading water and looking up at him. "There's something in here."

The other swimming children screamed and headed as fast as they could for the shore. Ned was frozen. Perhaps there were poisonous fish after all, and he was going to be responsible for the death of all these poor children. He felt as if he was going to faint. Suddenly a new girl popped out of the water, a girl Ned recognized from the Jarvises' farm.

"Hey! Ida! What are you doing down there?" Ned cried.

"Trying to get up there!"

The boy who had screamed glared at her. "You bit my leg!"

Ida swam toward the manor wall. "Yeah, well, it was in my way." She reached the wall, climbed up, and hoisted herself through the window. Inside, she tried to shake off the smelly water as if she were a Saint Bernard.

"I'm very happy to see you, Ida." Ned smiled hugely.

Ida looked at him. "Who the heck are you?"

"I'm Ned. I'm a friend of Josephine's."

"Where is she?"

"She's somewhere in here having dinner with the Master."

"You mean she's on his side?!"

"Yes, you could say that," a shrill voice behind them said. "But then, I consider everyone in Gulm to be on *my* side." Ned and Ida turned to see a black-haired boy with a nasty smile. He was followed by Fargus and an old man in an orange cap, who was pulling a tied-up Josephine behind him. The boy continued, "Now, I realize this a tender reunion but we have no time for salutations."

Ned gasped, "It's the Master." The boy looked exactly as Morgan had always described him, but, incredibly, he had not aged one day in twenty years. Just like Bruce's daughter, Sarah, and Ned's aunt, Lucy, the Master seemed incapable of getting older. Ned shuddered at the dark forces that must be at work in this manor.

Ida gaped at the oily boy with the smarmy grin. "You're the Master?" She gave out a snort. "And I'm the Princess of Cauliflower." The Master's smile disappeared.

Josephine tried to warn her. "Ida, don't—"

The Master stopped her. "Don't worry, Josephine. I'm used to this kind of rudeness. And it is an unpleasantness that Ida will experience herself soon enough."

Before anyone could ask what the Master meant, Ida marched toward him, red with anger. "I can't believe I spent all those years frightened of a scrawny brat with spotty skin! You're even shorter than I am! I'm going to wrestle you to the ground and make you eat dirt, you worthless little speck."

"I don't know what's happened to etiquette these days," the Master said calmly, and just as Ida was about to reach him, he brought his arm out from behind his back and revealed a large carving knife.

Ida stopped in her tracks. She looked at the knife and then at Fargus, who was trying to contain his excitement at seeing Ida alive.

The Master snickered, and the laugh echoed down the long silver tunnels of his manor. Surveying the children who had been trying to escape with Ned, the Master told them, "You will return to your rooms immediately." The children looked at Ned, waiting for instructions.

Ned nodded at them. "Go on." He looked at his aunt Lucy, still completely unaware of her surroundings. "Keep a close eye on Lucy."

They quietly obeyed, accustomed to the intense disappointment of life in the manor. Ida stayed her ground. "There are no Brothers in here to protect you. Why should we obey you?"

"Leverage, my girl. The world is all about leverage. And at this moment in time, I have something you want"—he grabbed Josephine and put the knife on her throat—"and you have nothing of interest to me. And that means . . . I win."

Ida spat, "The Brothers aren't even outside. Bruce led them into the forest to kill them. They're probably dead already."

The Master stared at her, a small twitch appearing in

his left eye. "Even if that were true, which I doubt, it is no longer of any consequence. I will soon have as many Brothers as I desire. Fargus has told me how."

Fargus stared at the floor in shame.

Ida smiled triumphantly. "No, he didn't. He can't even talk!"

The Master savored the moment. "I think you will find he is a chatty little thing, given the right motivation." He turned to Fargus. "Bind her hands, if you please, Fargus."

Fargus didn't move.

However, the Master knew how to motivate him. "Ah yes, quid pro quo—I quite forgot. Let's see, how about this, my dear boy? Many years ago a young couple who had been minding one of my lighthouses was brought to me— they had failed miserably. They'd cost me a ship and a great deal of silk, and I needed to recoup my losses. So I sold the couple to a tanner in the South. I believe the tanner's name was . . . oh dear, it has suddenly slipped my mind. Fargus, I am sure that if you were to tie up that impertinent little girl, I would be able to remember his name."

Ida stared at Fargus. "What's he talking about? You don't care about those people."

Fargus walked toward her, his left hand bandaged, his right hand carrying a rope. "He's talking about my parents. I'm sorry, Ida." Ida was so shocked to hear him speak that she didn't even struggle as he tied her.

FORTY-SEVEN

Bruce ran through the forest. Although the Brothers were tired, they were catching up to him, and they were enraged. They had been chasing various prey for hours without success, and they were ready for a kill. Bruce weaved in and out of the trees, jumping over fallen logs, wishing for the endurance of his youth. His plan was to keep running until nightfall, when the Brothers would have to return to the field and bury themselves under the old tree. He had considered running back to his property and locking himself in the house, but there was Alma to consider. She should be inside fixing dinner, but what if something pulled her outside? She might go to the garden to fetch a tomato or some rosemary. Alma might have kicked him out, but he didn't want to see her come to any harm.

And now that he had found Sarah, Alma would return to the woman she had once been, full of warmth and humor. He found strength in the vision of Alma and Sarah at his dinner table, a family once more. He was trying to remember the sound of Alma's laugh when his foot caught on a dead tree stump. He went flying and his head smacked against a rock. The world turned upside down and then spun over itself. Bruce couldn't move, but he could now hear Alma's laughter and he could see Sarah standing beside her, a fully grown beautiful woman with her whole life in front of her. Bruce smiled and let his mind drift toward them.

Seeing that their prey was immobilized, the Brothers stopped running. They circled him slowly, taunting him, as Bruce waited to see how they would do him in.

FORTY-EIGHT

Fargus finished tying Ida, trying not to cry out as his burned hand touched the rope, and then joined her to the rope that held Josephine. Ned saw their situation getting worse by the second.

"The Master's lying to you, Fargus," Josephine said quietly. "That's all he does—lie."

Fargus looked at her. "The Master won't hurt Ida. He promised me when I told him about the woodpile and the shed." He finished tying the knots.

The Master then instructed Fargus to tie Ned as well. Ned knew he could easily knock Fargus across the room, but he didn't want to hurt him and he didn't want to endanger Josephine. The Master was still holding the knife perilously close to her neck, and Josephine's eyes were wide with fright.

Josephine knew that Ned had his knife in its sheath

at the back of his belt. But to use it, he would need his hands free, so she had to stop Fargus from tying him up. Despite the blade at her throat, she blurted out, "Ida has been in the holes, Fargus. She's already hurt." Ida looked at her as if she were crazy. "She won't grow up. Just like the Master. She might feel older, but her body won't ever change."

Fargus turned toward the Master. "Is it true?"

"Well, it is more complicated than that. . . ."

"I SAID, IS IT TRUE?"

"I said she would stay alive, Fargus—I never said at what height."

Fargus felt the bile rise in his throat, just as it had when he had first met the Master. He looked down at the rope in his hands and glimpsed Ned's knife sitting in his belt. He looked at the Master and asked in an even voice, "What is the name of the tanner who bought my parents?"

The Master sensed he was losing control over the boy. "I can't recall it off the top of my head. I'll have to look it up in my library, as soon as these intruders are dealt with. So chop-chop, my boy."

Fargus ripped Ned's knife out of the sheath and walked menacingly toward the Master. The Master cackled, "Go ahead, boy! You've served your purpose!" He raised his carving knife in order to slice Fargus in two.

But as he went to bring the knife down, Josephine charged toward him. Her hands were tied but she still had her legs. Ida was forced to run with her, since they were tied together. Josephine jumped high and lifted her right foot, kicking the Master in the chest, knocking him backward and sending the knife flying from his grasp.

The Master was furious. He pointed to Josephine. "Seaworthy! Kill her!"

Josephine looked at the old servant, terrified.

But Mr. Seaworthy didn't budge.

"I order you, old man! Do it or face the consequences!"

But still Mr. Seaworthy did nothing. Instead, he turned to face Fargus, the one who was fated to take Mr. Seaworthy's place, who would be left to wander the halls of this dismal manor for the rest of his pointless life. Mr. Seaworthy croaked, "The tanner was called Arthur Torrence."

"Seaworthy!" The Master looked at him in shock and fury. "You'll pay for that!" He began to rise.

But as soon as Fargus heard the name of the tanner, the man who had bought his parents years ago, his body filled with a wild rage. He could hear and see nothing, just white. The world moved in slow motion, and he lurched forward and plunged the knife into the Master's heart.

Josephine screamed in horror, but Ida watched in shocked silence.

The Master fell onto the ground, stunned, a small whimper escaping his lips. He grasped his chest and reached out to Mr. Seaworthy for help, unable to draw air. He groaned and trembled and then, suddenly, he stopped breathing.

The room went silent.

Fargus seemed to wake from a dream. He looked down and saw the Master lying dead on the ground. He dropped the knife. *What have I done?*

Ned quickly unknotted the rope that bound Ida to Josephine. Ida walked over to the body of the Master, her hands still tied, and poked it with her toe. "That was really sick, Fargus!" And then she jumped back in disgust. The body at her feet was moving.

Ned cried, "Everyone get back!"

The Master was twitching.

"There's no blood!" Josephine noticed.

"He's not dead," said Mr. Seaworthy.

And sure enough, the Master began to convulse; his eyes flipped open, and he stared up in terror. Something very strange and very wrong was happening to his face. He was growing paler, if it was possible, and sprigs of facial hair were forming on his chin. And then, miraculously, his shoulders began to broaden. His legs grew longer and his hands doubled in size.

"What's happening?" Ned cried.

The Master began to laugh uncontrollably. "I'm aging! Finally! I can feel it!" The voice that emanated from him was deeper and richer than it had been before. Creases appeared on his forehead. He laughed again. "How do I look, Seaworthy?"

Mr. Seaworthy looked down in pity. "Very handsome, sir. A real man."

The Master smiled, and it was not a sneer or a smirk. It was a real smile, the first one Mr. Seaworthy had ever seen on the boy.

But suddenly the smile disappeared, as the Master realized that the aging wasn't slowing down. Wrinkles began to appear on his face, followed by age spots. In the space of seconds, his black hair turned gray and his hands shriveled with arthritis. He looked at Josephine in despair.

"Make it stop! Someone!"

Josephine went to him and knelt down, but there was nothing she knew how to do. So she took his hand and tried to comfort him.

A small pustule grew on his nose and burst, causing him to cry out in pain. A second one appeared on his cheek and *pop*. Soon his entire face was covered in rupturing pustules, and then his whole body.

Josephine closed her eyes, unable to watch the horror, but she could still hear him scream as they burst. She wished she were anywhere else in the world but here.

When she opened her eyes, the room had gone still. It seemed the Master's pain had ended. He lay there unmoving, looking more old and frail than Mr. Seaworthy.

Josephine bent over his chest to see if he was still breathing, and the body jumped slightly.

"Stand back, Josephine. He's not done!" Ned warned.

Josephine released his hand.

And then, as strangely as it had begun, the aging process began to reverse itself. The Master's hair turned black once more, the wrinkles disappeared, his body grew smaller, and he quickly became the boy they had all known.

But it didn't stop there.

He was an eight-year-old boy. Then seven. Then six.

"Make it stop, Seaworthy! I order you to help me!" his three-year-old self squealed.

Then he became an innocent toddler, sucking his thumb, and then, finally, he became a small baby, curled into a little ball, playing with his feet.

"Is it over?" Josephine asked, peeking through her fingers and the rope that bound her hands.

No one could answer, because no one knew. But as they waited, the baby stayed the same, gurgling and smiling up at them.

The Master's transformation appeared to be complete.

Mr. Seaworthy picked up the baby, wrapping him in his uniform jacket. "I suggest you move on as quickly as possible. The other servants will be here shortly."

Ned nodded, still unable to comprehend what he'd just seen. "What's going to happen to him?"

Mr. Seaworthy held the baby against his chest. "I'll look after him, as I always have."

Ida was having none of it. "But he'll just grow up and start taking children again!"

"Don't worry, child," assured Mr. Seaworthy. "This time I'll make sure that the boy gets what he never had."

"Love," Josephine said.

Mr. Seaworthy nodded. "You take care of the other children."

Ida wasn't entirely satisfied that they should leave the Master alive at all, but she knew they needed to get moving. "That was the most disgusting thing I've ever seen. It was great! Don't you think, Fargus? Fargus?" She looked around and Fargus was nowhere to be found. "Where'd he go?"

Ned said, "He probably went to tell the other children we can leave. Let's find them and get out of here."

Ned was untying the girls' wrists when Josephine saw something on the ground. When she got closer, she saw that it was the piece of lava stone that the Master had always kept in his pocket. "Step on it, Ned! Grind it into a million pieces!"

Ned didn't question her. He stomped on the stone again and again until it had crumbled to dust.

"Thank you," Josephine said. "Now the Master can never control the Brothers again."

FORTY-NINE

The three of them—Ned, Josephine, and Ida—then ran down the halls, opening all the silver doors and releasing everyone. Ned found Lucy and picked her up in his arms. Josephine helped gather the rest and led them toward the front door.

Ida searched for Fargus in vain, checking every room twice, joining the others only after Josephine convinced her that Fargus must have already left the manor.

The group went spilling out the front door and over the drawbridge. Outside, the light was just starting to fade. The children ran into the field, careful to avoid the feeding holes, breathing in their freedom.

Ida saw the wet group of escaped children who had crossed the moat earlier. They were huddled together for warmth. She ran over to them. "Did any of you see a boy run out here?"

"Don't tell her anything. She bit me," the boy from the water said.

"Get over it, salmon breath," Ida responded. "Did you see him?"

A girl with moat scum in her hair answered, "Yeah, I saw him. He looked like he was going to spew."

"Thank you." Ida walked over to Ned and Josephine. "He's around here somewhere," she told them, as if they had been worried sick and not her.

Josephine turned toward Ned and for the first time noticed the weak girl leaning against him. Something about her was eerily familiar. "Is that . . . ?"

"Yes," he said. "This is my father's sister, Lucy."

"Wow. Hello, Lucy, my name's Josephine."

Lucy stared into space.

Ned patted her head and explained, "She's confused. And she has no idea who I am."

Josephine remembered the locket. "I might have something that will help." She took off the necklace Morgan had given her and handed it to Ned.

Ned opened up the locket, showing the pictures inside to Lucy. There was his father, a cocky teenager, and Lucy, eyes bright and full of humor.

"Lucy, do you remember this? This is *you* . . . and this is my dad, Morgan." She stared at it blankly. But after a few moments something seemed to stir behind her eyes.

"Morgan," Ned repeated. "Your brother."

"Mooorgaaan," she said slowly, tasting the name on her lips.

Josephine tried to help. "Lucy, do you remember *The Dancing Possum*? It was your favorite book!"

Lucy smiled slightly. "Possum," she repeated.

"Yeah! That's right! *The Dancing Possum!*" Ned laughed.

"I think the necklace belongs to her now," Josephine told Ned, and he happily placed it over Lucy's head. Lucy held on to the locket tightly.

Suddenly Fargus appeared out of nowhere. He looked pale and sickly as he approached. Ida ran to him.

"Where'd you go? Are you all right?"

He grinned weakly. "I got sick . . . in the moat . . . I didn't want you to see."

"Oh. Are you finished now?"

He nodded.

Ida put her arm around his shoulder and led him over to Josephine and the others. She announced to all the children, "Fargus destroyed the Master! He's a hero!"

The children cheered and clapped for Fargus, who was mortified that he could be celebrated for doing something so horrid. Josephine and Ned couldn't bring themselves to clap, having seen what had happened to the Master.

Ida told him, "You did okay in there. If it were me,

I would've stabbed the Master in the eyeballs, but you did your best." She looked down and for the first time noticed Fargus's bandaged hand. "What happened?"

Fargus replied, "The Master . . . he . . . I burned it. That's all."

"Disgusting! Can I see?"

He slowly unwrapped the bandage and revealed his charred flesh. His hand looked as if it had been replaced by a melting wax replica.

"Oh, Fargus!" Josephine said with pity, tears welling in her eyes. "You must be in horrible pain."

"It's not so bad," he lied. "It just hurts when the air hits it."

Josephine remembered the gloves in her pocket. She took them out and handed them to Fargus. "Here. Take these."

"I just need the one," Fargus said, gladly taking the glove.

"Then you'll look crazy," Ida said. "Better to wear both and have people think you're just cold."

Fargus was in no mood to fight with her, so he put both gloves on.

"Ned, do you have—?" But Josephine didn't finish the sentence.

A sour look had appeared on Ned's face. "Do you smell that?"

And suddenly the others could smell it too—garbage and herbs—and as they recognized the odor, they began to panic. "The Brothers! They're coming!" Josephine cried. She surveyed the field and the edges of the forest, waiting for the horrible grunting beasts to show themselves.

"We have nowhere to run," Ned said.

"Stay together!" Josephine ordered. Otherwise they would be picked off one by one.

A girl screamed and pointed. Josephine saw the trees parting, and she began to scream herself as she saw both Brothers heading straight for them.

Everyone made a run for it without any thought or reason, just sprinting as fast as their legs could carry them. "No!" Josephine cried. "Stay together!"

And then she decided to run too, but Ned grabbed her arm so she couldn't move. "What are you doing?!" she screamed.

"Wait!" he cried. "Do you see what I see?"

Josephine thought Ned had lost his mind, but when she looked back at the Brothers, she, too, saw something strange. Someone appeared to be *riding* one of them. "Who is that?" she asked incredulously.

"I'm not sure," Ned said, "but . . . I think it might be . . . BRUCE!"

"Bruce?" Josephine squinted her eyes, and sure

enough, she could make out the tall figure of Bruce sitting on top of one of the Brothers. And he was grinning from ear to ear.

Ned shook his head in disbelief. "That's the most unlikely thing I've ever seen."

Seeing Bruce's blissful expression, Josephine decided there was nothing to fear. "Bruce!" she shouted, and waved.

Bruce waved back, and then suddenly a brown-haired girl in the group yelled, "Poppa!"

Ned told Josephine, "That's Sarah, Bruce and Alma's daughter."

Bruce and the Brothers headed for Sarah. When they got close to her, the Brother Bruce was riding sat down and allowed Bruce to slide off his back.

Bruce ran and scooped Sarah up in his arms. "I thought I'd never see you again!" she cried.

The Brothers calmly observed the whole proceeding. They lay down in the field and one even scratched his belly.

Josephine and Ned came running, as did all the other children. They were amazed to see the Brothers being docile, but no one dared get too close to them.

Once Josephine reached Bruce, she could see that he was a mess. His face was bruised and bloodied and he had a huge scratch running down his arm.

All the children yelled at once: "Bruce! Bruce!" "What happened?" "Are you okay?" "How did you do it?" "What happened to the Brothers?"

Bruce laughed and put Sarah down. "Well, it was the darnedest thing. I was running through the forest as fast as I could, but the Brothers were gaining on me. I'm not as quick as I used to be, and I tripped and fell, and, well, I was sure I was a goner. And one of them—I call him Blacky—was just about to tear me apart, I'd say, when all of a sudden he stopped. I mean, he just stopped dead in his tracks and shook his head as if he were waking up out of a bad dream or something. And all the anger and savagery just seemed to drain out of him.

"It's hard to describe, but all at once he reminded me of a new calf who'd lost his way. So that's how I treated him. I pet his head a little and used a soft voice, and next thing I knew, he and the other one—I call him Smoky—were as sweet as kittens."

Josephine blurted, "It must have been when Ned stepped on the lava stone! The Master had been using it to control the Brothers!"

"Where is the Master?" Bruce asked.

"It's a long story," Josephine answered. "But we don't need to worry about him anymore."

Bruce grinned and hugged Sarah again.

Josephine watched the Brothers grooming themselves

and felt a surge of pity. "Poor things," she said. She crept closer to them, and, for the first time she noticed that indeed one was inky black and the other was a more smoky gray color. She approached Blacky and, to the other children's amazement, began to pet the long spikes on the creature's back. They were coarse, but she found if she stroked down, the way the spikes were lying, they were not unpleasant to the touch. Blacky sighed with pleasure at her touch. "They were just being treated badly, that's all. Maybe they just miss their mother."

"If those are children, then I'd hate to see the parents!" Ned cracked.

"Ned, you're brilliant!" Josephine said. "The Brothers need to go home to their parents. I can take them with me! Back through one of Brokhun's Cracks."

"But," Ida asked, "how can you be sure it will lead them home?"

"Morgan said it would take you wherever you needed to go," Josephine answered. "And the Master told me that in their own world they don't need to feed off children."

Bruce nodded in approval. "Then it has to be done. They deserve to go home, just like the rest of us."

One of the children yelled, "*We* want to go home!"

Others soon joined in. "Back to Gulm!" "Let's go!" "Who knows the way?"

Josephine looked at her friends, and they all knew it was time to say good-bye. She said to Bruce, "Thank you for everything. You were wonderful." She stood on tiptoe and he bent down to meet her, and she kissed his cheek.

He blushed with pride. "Just be gentle with Smoky and Blacky," he said, "and they'll do everything you ask." Josephine glanced at the Brothers and hoped Bruce was right.

Ida punched Bruce in the arm, startling him. "Thanks for helping me out of that hole."

"It was the least I could do," he answered. "It was my fault you and the boy were with the Master in the first place." He grabbed Sarah's hand and said, "Josephine, I'll leave you in Ned's capable hands. I hope you find your way home. You've earned it." Bruce then turned to the big group of children. "Follow me if you want to go to Gulm!"

He headed for the forest with the children running after him, making sure no one was left behind. Ned and his aunt Lucy were still standing with Josephine.

Ned looked apologetic. "I think I need to get Lucy home as soon as possible."

Josephine nodded. "Of course. Don't worry about me. I've got the Brothers to protect me."

Ned nodded and reached into his bag, pulling out the claganmeter still carefully wrapped in cloth.

"It seems to have stayed dry," he told her. "It's really simple to use. Just keep a close eye on both clocks, and if they ever tell you different times, you know you're in the right place." He handed it to her. "Are you sure you're okay by yourself?"

"Yes, and thank you," she said.

"If it doesn't work, the door or crack or whatever, you can always . . . uh . . . come back to Gulm. Now that the Master is gone, it should be a pretty decent place to live."

Josephine beamed at the invitation, and she found herself very tempted to stay. "Tell Morgan thank you for everything. I don't know what I would've done if you two hadn't found me."

"Morgan?" Lucy said. "I want to see Morgan!"

Ned smiled at her. "Yes. We're going to see him now." He hugged Josephine with great affection, and then he and Lucy went running after Bruce and the others.

Josephine turned to Fargus and Ida, ready to make them a proposition. "Ned's father showed me how to find the door back home. If you wanted . . . since you don't have any family here . . . you *could* come home with me." She tried not to show how much it would mean to her to keep them in her life.

Fargus looked torn. "I want to go, really," he said, "but I have to find that man Arthur Torrence. What if my parents are still alive?" His eyes shone with the possibility.

"And if this pea brain is going to go running all over the South," Ida added, "I better go look after him." Ida wouldn't meet Josephine's gaze.

Josephine thought she knew what was bothering Ida. "I'm sorry about what I said about you not growing up. I was just trying to distract Fargus. I don't know if it's true."

Ida chewed on the inside of her lip for a moment. "I think it's a bunch of mice droppings."

But Josephine knew Ida well enough by now to know she was lying.

"And even if it is true, big deal! Adults are a bunch of morons."

Fargus laughed. But Josephine didn't. She didn't think there was anything funny about not growing up. She had dreamed her whole life of becoming an adult, leaving her father's house, and starting her own life. She didn't know what she would do if something took that away.

Josephine thought she saw a small tear welling in the corner of Ida's eye, but the girl turned away. "Let's get going, Fargus, before the sun goes down."

Josephine gave Ida a big hug, crying out, "I hope I see you again."

Ida turned red and pulled away quickly. "Okay. And . . . uh . . ." Ida stumbled over her words, which Josephine had never witnessed before. "I guess I should say . . . thank you . . . and everything . . . for coming back for us."

Josephine smiled. "Of course I came back. You're my friends."

Fargus used his good hand to touch Josephine's arm. He whispered, "I'm sorry I dragged you into all of this."

"I wouldn't have missed it for the world," she whispered back.

Ida, who no longer wanted to be a part of this sentimental parting, pulled Fargus away and began marching him purposefully south.

Josephine waved good-bye, and as she watched a grinning Fargus wave back at her with his gloved hand, she suddenly felt very strange. She felt the way one does when one has forgotten a dream, but then something in real life suddenly reminds one of that dream, and the whole night's adventure comes rushing back like a wave.

Josephine felt the need to return home immediately.

FIFTY

Nowadays, if one asks the people of Gulm about the night the children came home, one will get many versions of the story. Some will say it was early morning and others will say it was the dead of night. Some will say it was raining, while many claim it was the clearest night they'd ever seen. The part they *can* agree upon is this:

The people of Gulm were in their beds, tossing and turning, unable to sleep, as they had been for twenty years, when they heard a rustling outside. Some of the older folk thought it was just a strong wind. Whatever it was, it went racing through the alleyways like a bubbling brook. The people were afraid and they bolted their doors, convinced it was soldiers or, worse yet, a plague.

And then the knocking began.

Someone, something, was knocking on all of their doors. The women screamed and the men pushed them back into the bedrooms for safety, even while their own knees were shaking.

Later Louise Millamud claimed it was she who opened the door first, but everyone knew her for a coward. Edwin Starch said he was the one. He explained that he was right up against his door, with his ear against the wood, listening to the sound of the bubbling brook whooshing by, when he began to suspect that it was not water at all but voices. And then he concentrated harder and realized that the bubbling voices were actually people giggling. Convinced he was going mad, he flung open the door, shaking a large rake over his head.

But instead of the devil he expected, he saw children. Dozens of them, running through the streets, knocking on doors. He had to rub his eyes, because for a moment he thought he saw little Ignatius Powell from next door, unchanged from the day he'd been taken. He called out to him and the boy waved.

Edwin was sure he was dreaming and was ready to poke himself with his rake when his own son arrived—a gangly boy with protruding ears. Georgie Starch. Edwin placed his hands upon his own face to feel the wrinkles that the past twenty years had brought, wondering if maybe he had gone back in time. And then his wife screamed. She had tiptoed up behind him and had seen Georgie standing outside. While her husband was frozen in shock, Hattie Starch ran straight out to the boy and threw her arms around him.

And this scene was repeated up and down every street of the town. Mothers sobbed and smothered their lost children into their bosoms. Fathers stood agape, quiet tears running down their cheeks, as they waited for a turn to touch their rescued sons and daughters. Orphaned children from the Institute remained with friends they had made in the manor and were welcomed into local families as if they were their own. Word spread quickly of the demise of the Master. Angus the bellman ran up the tower and swung back and forth on the rope connected to the bells, filling the air with triumphant chimes.

Ned walked through the throngs of ecstatic reunions, Lucy walking beside him. He had never seen such emotion. He looked at his neighbors, people he had known these many years, and saw color returning to their cheeks. For the first time in Ned's life, laughter filled the streets.

He and Lucy found their way to the alley that led to his apartment. Ned had never been happier to see his front door. Lucy stood beside him, timid but more lucid than when he had found her. He fumbled with his keys, hands shaking with anticipation. He felt the click of the last lock and pushed open the door.

"Father!" he yelled, but there was no one there. "Hello?" he tried again. "Dad, where are you? I have a surprise!"

But Morgan was nowhere to be seen. Ned's heart sank. "Come on in," he told Lucy. "You can sit wherever you like." She followed him in and tried not to show her immense disappointment that Morgan wasn't there. She asked to use the bathroom and Ned pointed the way.

Ned was perplexed. Where could Morgan be? He started to worry. He knew that Morgan had not expected him to ever return. What if he had done something stupid?

At that moment the front door opened and there stood Morgan, in his best suit, with a stupid lopsided grin on his face. At first, Ned thought maybe he was drunk. But then, to Ned's horror, he saw the reason for his father's gaiety. Beatrice was right behind him, and she was wearing . . . a wedding dress!

"Dad!" Ned cried.

"Neddy?" Morgan looked at him in shock and then delight and then anger. "What are you doing here? You promised me you would go with Josephine to safety!"

"But Dad—"

"No buts, Ned. You LIED to me."

"I lied to you? What about her?" He pointed to Beatrice. "What's going on?"

Morgan looked at Beatrice, grinned, and said to Ned sheepishly, "After you left, I finally understood that life is short. And it's too short to live alone. So I asked Beatrice to marry me."

Ned slapped his forehead with his hand. At that moment, Lucy emerged from the bathroom. Morgan and Beatrice turned in alarm toward the stranger.

"Who's that?" Morgan demanded.

"I've been trying to tell you, but you've been too busy with your stupid nuptials!"

"Trying to tell me what?"

"The Master . . . he's gone. And so are the Brothers. And this here . . . this is Lucy."

It was too much information for Morgan to absorb all at once. He looked at the little girl standing in his living room. "That's madness, Ned! How could this child possibly be my—?" But he stopped short and looked at her again.

She had dirty blond hair and freckles and the same look his sister used to get when she woke out of a nightmare. Morgan felt as if he were seeing a ghost. "What *is* this? Where did you—how did she—" but he couldn't finish. He ran to Lucy, picked her up, and twirled her in his arms.

"Lucy! Lucy! Is it really you?"

"Put me down, Morgan!" she cried. She sounded much older than the Lucy he remembered and he put her down immediately.

She grabbed a chair to get her balance back. "I don't know what the fuss is about," she said. "I haven't changed one lick. You're the one who's become as old as Father!" Morgan laughed, amazed to hear her voice. Lucy put her tiny arms around his neck and hugged him furiously. "I've never been happier to see anyone in my whole life."

Beatrice cleared her throat, and Morgan remembered she was there. "Lucy, I would like you to meet my new wife, Beatrice."

"New is right," Ned cracked. "Less than an hour, by my reckoning."

"Ned! Don't be rude!" Lucy admonished. She walked over to Beatrice and gave her a hug too. "Lovely to meet you. I am Morgan's sister, Lucy."

"Sister?" Beatrice asked, befuddled.

Ned sighed, realizing that fighting the inclusion of Beatrice into his family would be futile. "Why don't I make some tea and explain it all to you."

Everyone nodded, but Beatrice said, "No, I'll make the tea. Ned, you sit down and tell your father what's happened before the poor man has a heart attack."

Ned looked at Morgan, and sure enough, he looked a bit green.

"You okay, Dad?"

"Am I okay? In one day my son has returned, my sister is back from the dead, and I got married. I've never been better in my life!"

Ned laughed and sat down, ready to tell his father, his aunt, and his new stepmother all about his adventure.

FIFTY-ONE

Back at the Institute, Kitchen Maggie and Stairway Ruth were just sitting down to dinner. They sat together at the far end of the long dining room table, staring at the empty chairs that used to teem with orphans. Ruth picked at her pigeon stew. It was the fifth time they had eaten stew this week, and her stomach churned at the idea of eating it yet again.

Maggie, on the other hand, happily slurped away, spraying broth and gristle all over her many chins. Ruth glared at her in disgust and hatred when suddenly the front door of the Institute came crashing open.

Maggie's head shot up from her stew and she saw her worst nightmare come to life: One of the Brothers was *entering the building*!

She shrieked at the top of her lungs, while Ruth leaped from her seat and tried to hide under the table, hoping that the Brother might choose to make a meal out of Maggie first.

The mammoth creature lumbered into the dining room and its stench filled the air.

"Ruth! He's finally done it! The Master has sent the Brothers to kill us!" Maggie screeched and ran into the kitchen.

From where Ruth trembled under the table, she could see that the situation had worsened: The second Brother had now entered the Institute. She felt faint. And then the strangest thing happened. She heard a girl's voice. "Come out, Stairway Ruth. We can see you!"

Ruth, her pointy knees shaking, crawled out from under the table, and when she looked up, she saw Josephine sitting astride one of the Brothers.

"You!" Ruth cried.

"Yes, me," Josephine said, triumphant. "I'm back!"

Ruth attempted a smile (something she had not done on purpose in at least fifty years). "I'm so relieved you are safe, child. We are happy to welcome you back to the Institute and we hope—"

Josephine waved her off with her hand. "Stop talking, please. That's not why we're here."

"Oh? Why, then, are you here, sweet, sweet girl?" Ruth simpered. "Are you working for the Master now?"

Josephine was suddenly inspired. "Yes, that's right!

I'm working for the Master. And he has orders for you both!"

Ruth nodded. "Of course, anything. Anything!"

Josephine's brain twirled with possibilities and she was positively giddy with power. "The Master has declared that you and Kitchen Maggie shall be the new town sweepers of Gulm, but you are not to tell anyone. It is to be a secret, forever!"

Ruth nodded. "Yes, a secret."

"This is a special assignment and you must never speak of it."

"Never," Ruth repeated.

"The current sweepers, Morgan and his son, are never to lift a finger ever again. Before they arrive to work every day, you will have already swept and polished every cobblestone in Gulm. Do you understand?"

"Yes, yes, I understand, but why—?"

"Enough!" Josephine yelled. "Don't test the Master's patience!"

"No, never. Tell the Master he is very magnanimous indeed."

"Now go!" Josephine pointed to the front door.

"But I n-need to—" Ruth stammered.

"NOW. Or suffer the consequences!" Josephine bellowed.

Ruth squeaked and ran out the front door as fast as her pigeon-filled body would take her.

Josephine giggled and steered the Brother, Blacky, toward the kitchen. He was so large that he crushed all the chairs in his path. Smoky joined them, crushing the table into tinder.

The door to the kitchen was small, so Blacky just knocked down the entire wall. When the dust settled, they could see Kitchen Maggie trying to climb into her pantry, which was only big enough to hold one of her beefy legs. As she saw the Brothers storm the kitchen, she screamed, "Get back! I've got a butcher knife, you brutes!"

"The Master has ordered you to Gulm," Josephine told her matter-of-factly. "Stairway Ruth has your instructions. If you start running now, you just might catch her."

Maggie looked at her, bug-eyed, not sure if she should trust the girl. But anything was better than facing the Brothers, so she squeezed her enormous frame past Blacky and Smoky and went shrieking out the front door after Stairway Ruth. "Wait for meeeee!"

"Well done, boys," Josephine chuckled. "I can walk from here." Blacky sat on the floor and Josephine slid down his back. It had been an easy ride, like riding Mabel, if a bit more smelly. "We have to go down there now." She pointed to the cellar.

She opened the door. The cellar appeared to be exactly the same as it had been when she'd left. She couldn't believe it. It felt so long ago that she had first arrived here. She felt like a completely different person from the girl who had hid behind the flour sacks from Ida.

She walked down the stairs, and when she looked back, she could see that the passageway was much too small for the Brothers, but they didn't hesitate for a moment. They crashed through the wall and leaped onto the cellar floor. Josephine could see that they were as eager to get home as she was.

She walked to the center of the room and took the claganmeter out of her pocket. She unfolded it and held it out before her as she had seen Morgan do. She looked at both clocks. They were in perfect synchronicity. She slowly began walking around the room, keeping her eyes locked on the second hands of the two clocks. But she saw no change.

She felt a moment of doubt, but then she remembered something. "The woodpile!" Fargus had said he'd been hiding behind the woodpile when he'd found the passage! Her heart pounded as she looked at the woodpile in the corner. She approached it, expecting to see something strange, but it looked like every other pile of wood she'd ever seen. She circled it and saw nothing peculiar on the other side, either. She held up the claganmeter.

She watched it for a full minute, the second hands still ticking together perfectly, when all of a sudden, it was as if the clock on the right hiccuped: The minute hand jumped backward instead of forward! Josephine's heart leaped. She checked again, and sure enough, the clock on the right was now running about two seconds behind the clock on the left. She marked the exact spot with a stick from the woodpile.

She then grabbed a second stick and tossed it toward the spot. And suddenly it was as if a thunderstorm had hit the cellar. Wind whipped through the air and there was a bolt of light and a horrible cracking sound, and the wooden stick was gone—sucked right into the hole.

"Blacky! Quick! I've found it!" she exclaimed.

The Brother came running but was blocked by the woodpile. He lifted a mighty claw and sent the logs flying across the room. Josephine ducked, and when she looked up, he was gazing at her questioningly.

"You two go first," she said. "You should go together. Just think about home and your mother, and you'll get back to her."

He tilted his head at her, and Josephine felt that he understood. He turned toward his brother and snorted at him twice. Smoky walked up next to him and he, too, tilted his head at Josephine, as if in thanks.

"Here," she said. "It's right here," and she pointed to the spot where the stick had disappeared.

Blacky took a step toward Josephine and nuzzled her with his nose. She was thoroughly disgusted as she felt his snot on her neck, but she knew he meant it as affection, so she didn't pull away. She stroked his neck and said, "I'll miss you, too."

When he had finished, he looked at his brother, and the two of them clomped into the spot Josephine had marked. Again, wind blew through the cellar, a light flashed and popped, and the Brothers were swallowed into a void.

Josephine couldn't believe it! She had felt it happen to herself, but it was another thing altogether to see it from the outside. She just hoped that the Brothers ended up in a good place.

Now it was her turn. She took a deep breath and thought of her house, her collection of books, and her father—his stern, stubborn face that she knew and loved.

And she stepped forward into the wind and the light.

FIFTY-TWO

Josephine landed with a hard thud. She was disoriented and for a moment forgot what she was doing. But she looked up and saw the interior of the shed, and she knew she had made it home. She jumped to her feet and flew out the door, then stopped dead in her tracks. Sitting outside not four feet from the shed door was her father, asleep in an armchair that was normally in the living room.

"Father?" she blurted.

He sprang up with his arms raised, ready to fight. "Wha—?" he exclaimed.

Josephine recoiled. Mr. Russing spun around, blinking and confused. His eyes finally settled on Josephine, and his face contorted.

"Josephine?" he managed.

"Yes, sir," she answered, surprised to hear him speak

directly to her. Her hand automatically reached up to smooth her hair down. She could only imagine what she looked like with her dirt-streaked face, muddy dress, and gloveless hands.

He gaped at her, and Josephine squirmed under his gaze, her heart still racing from her journey.

After a long silence her father twisted his face again and sputtered, "Y-y-you're back."

Josephine couldn't tell if there was relief or disappointment in his voice, so she only replied, "Yes."

He approached her and put his hand on her back, giving her a little push in the direction of the house. She obeyed and began walking toward the back porch. Josephine felt all the excitement and energy of her adventure being sucked out of her.

So this was the way it would be: exactly as it had been before.

She marched up the porch steps and into the kitchen, where her father pointed to her chair at the dinner table. Josephine plopped down and stared at him. There was an added stiffness to Mr. Russing, a tension that filled his body. Was it anger?

Josephine suddenly felt nervous. Perhaps she was in trouble for having skipped school. Or maybe her father thought she had run away. She began to blabber. "It was an accident, really. I didn't mean to leave, I didn't mean to go—"

"Shh," her father warned as he put the kettle on the stove. Josephine sighed and put her head down on the table. She felt tears beginning to burn. She already missed Ida and Fargus. She bet that Ida would have known what to say right now. And Fargus might have even run up and kicked her father in the leg. The thought made the corners of her mouth turn up.

Her father caught the look and said, "What's that? Why are you smiling?"

She looked up and replied, "Nothing, sir."

He then asked forcefully, "Are you hurt?"

She shook her head, realizing that he'd asked a question about her. *He is actually worried about me.* She felt desperate to keep him talking.

"No, Father. I'm not hurt. How are you?"

He seemed surprised at the question. "I'm fine, Josephine. Fine."

She tried to explain herself again. "I went away, but I didn't mean to. I'm sorry if I—"

"I know," he interrupted.

He knows? How could he possibly know?

Once again Josephine felt dread in her belly. It was the same feeling of dread she'd experienced the first time she'd heard the Master's full name: Leopold Reginald Russing, the same name as her father. She'd never been able to figure out how it could've happened. She could admit to herself now that somewhere in the back of her head she'd been terrified that her father *was* the Master. But now she knew that was impossible. She had met the Master, and he was just a young boy, destined to stay a child forever. That is, until Fargus stabbed him and he became a baby again. She wondered if that baby would be able to grow up normally. If so, then . . . perhaps . . .

Josephine's heart stopped. Her father. That baby, the Master, had grown up to be her father!

She heard screaming in her head. She wanted to throw up. Her father removed the steaming teakettle from the stove and the shrieking ceased. Josephine watched as he took teacups out of the cupboard, as if everything was normal. But her world was falling apart.

That was why they shared the same name. She had to escape. She had to run away from their house and never come back. She still had the claganmeter. If only she could reach the shed before he caught up with her.

Mr. Russing set a cup of tea in front of her, and before she could reconsider, Josephine threw the hot liquid at him and went sprinting out the back door. She could hear him scream, "Josephine! Wait!"

She crossed the yard in seconds and flung open the

shed door. She fumbled in her pocket for the clagan-meter and finally managed to grasp it. She waved it around the shed frantically but couldn't see any difference in the two clocks. She needed to move it slower but she didn't have time. Her father's voice was getting closer.

"Josephine! Stop! Let me explain!" he bellowed.

One of the clock hands seemed to jump a little bit and Josephine knew she'd found the right spot. But her mind was blank. She couldn't think of where she wanted to go. She was frozen.

Suddenly, her father's large hand reached around her waist and lifted her up. She struggled against his grip as he carried her, kicking and screaming, out of the shed.

She kicked and spat and clawed at him, determined to get free. He tightened his grip and dragged her back toward the house.

This is it, she thought. *Now that I know his secret, he can't let me live.* Josephine looked down, grabbed his gloved hand, and bit as hard as she could. He howled in pain and loosened his grip. It was just enough for Josephine to wrestle free.

As she hit the ground, she jumped away from him and then whirled around, seething with anger. "It's you! You're the Master! You hurt all those children and now you're going to hurt me!"

"No, no!" her father cried. "You don't understand."

"I understand that you're a MONSTER!" she shrieked. She shook her fist at him and realized she was holding his silk glove. She looked at him. He was no longer trying to grab her, but was nursing his hand where she had bit it. Josephine realized she was looking, for the first time in her life, at Leopold Russing's bare hand.

It took her several seconds to register what she was looking at. His left hand was hideously burned.

Josephine didn't understand what she was seeing. "Your hand! But it's just like . . . ." She looked up at his face, which was full of desperation. "Fargus's hand."

He nodded meekly. "That's what I've been trying to tell you."

The world began to spin and Josephine felt the blood pounding in her ears. What did this mean? Did he . . . was he . . . ? Her brain seemed to short-circuit and pop, and she collapsed into a heap on the grass.

It was several minutes later when she came to, and she was propped up in the armchair next to the shed. Her father was hovering over her with a glass of water. "Josephine . . . are you all right? Josephine?"

She could barely speak and her mind was reeling. He held the glass toward her and forced a sip of water between her lips. "Drink this. It will make you feel better."

She felt the cold liquid run down her throat and then began to remember what had been happening before she'd fainted. She gaped at her father. "You . . . were trying to tell me . . . something."

He knelt next to her and took a deep breath. "Yes. I was trying to say that my real name is Fargus Dudson, and . . . I was born in Gulm." He paused, letting it all sink in.

Josephine shook her head and pushed the water glass away. "No. It's impossible. I don't believe you!" She felt ready to run from him again.

Her father sighed, not sure what to do next. "How else could I have known where to wait for you?"

Josephine looked down at the armchair her father had dragged from the living room out to the shed.

He continued, "As a boy, I found my way to you through this shed, and I hoped that was how you would find your way back to me now. I've been sleeping here, eating here, waiting for you to come home."

She studied his features as if for the first time—the thin lips, small chin, and little cowlick at the back of his head. She looked deep into his hard brown eyes, and suddenly, as if hit by a mallet, she knew he was telling the truth.

But how was it possible? "Fargus is younger than I am!"

"Yes, I was. But that was fifty years ago."

Fifty years? She had gone back in time *fifty* years? "You mean, the shed took me to another world *and* another time?" This time/space continuum thing was proving to be even more complex than Morgan had told her.

"Brokhun's Cracks remain a mystery, but I believe they take you wherever you need to go."

"*Need* to go? But why did I need to go *there?*"

"To *save* us, of course—me and Ida." He stood. "Why don't you come with me back to the kitchen. I'll make you some new tea."

Josephine blanched. "The tea! I threw it at you!"

"Luckily you've got bad aim." He offered her his hand, which was once again covered with his gray glove, and she allowed him to help her up.

Moments later the two of them were sitting face-to-face at the kitchen table. Her father looked her straight in the eye, something she was unaccustomed to. He had agreed to answer any questions she asked. She was so full of them, she thought she'd explode.

"If you knew I was going to go to Gulm, why didn't you warn me?"

"I *didn't* know. For me, it's been a lifetime since I left you standing in front of the Master's manor. I didn't understand the truth until after you went missing. You weren't in the house and you'd skipped school. So I searched your room, and I found the brown case with that old photograph inside, and I finally understood that you were the girl who had come to the Institute to rescue me and Ida."

"But . . . why didn't you come to help me? The Brothers almost got me, the Master almost stabbed me . . . I could've died!"

"But that wasn't what happened—it wasn't meant to be. You *saved* us."

Josephine's heart sank. He hadn't really been worried about her at all. He'd just been worried about his own skin. She whispered, "So you were just worried about you and Ida."

"No! I was afraid if I interfered at all with the past that I'd put *you* in danger. My presence might have thrown everything off course." The concern and anxiety in his voice were genuine. "I've been worried sick, waiting for you to get back. Can you forgive me for being so ignorant?"

Josephine was torn between distrusting the stern man who had ignored her all these years and believing her sweet friend Fargus who had never lied to her. She decided to trust her friend and nodded her head.

Her father exhaled in relief.

Josephine pressed on to the next urgent thought on her mind. "Where's Ida?"

Her father sighed. "I don't know. After we said good-bye to you, we traveled south. Every town we passed through, we asked about a tanner named Torrence, but no one had heard of him, so we just kept moving. This went on and on, but while I was growing older and becoming a teenager, Ida stayed exactly the same, just like all the other children who'd gone into the holes. She'd never have admitted it, but she was tortured by it. She was always searching for a cure. One day she heard about a possible remedy that was in a distant country, and she told me she needed to go find it. I was still looking for my parents, so she went without me."

"And that was it? You never saw her again?" Josephine was immensely disappointed.

He looked mournful. "No. But I think of her often."

"Did you find your parents?"

Mr. Russing proceeded to tell her about his years searching far and wide for his mother and father. It was a tragic tale. By the time he'd found the tanner who'd bought his parents from the Master, his mother had died from exhaustion and his father, heartbroken, had drowned himself in the tannery pits.

Josephine felt tears run down her cheeks. "That's so sad."

"That's when I decided I needed to change my name, make a new start. There'd been a lot of gossip about what had happened to the Russing family and their fortune. The Master had left his hometown as a boy and no one had heard from him since. His estate lay unclaimed. I decided that he still owed me for the death of my parents, so I went to Drubshire and claimed that I was his son. I sold his home and belongings and left that place a rich man. I traveled back to the Institute and used one of Brokhun's Cracks to get here, and I continued living as Leopold Reginald Russing. Fargus was dead as far as I was concerned."

Now that her father was sharing his life with her, Josephine felt emboldened. "Father, why don't you ever talk about Mother? Why don't you ever talk at all?"

His voice trembled a little. "She was the best thing that had ever happened to me, and after she died, it was like she took my voice with her, just like after my parents were arrested."

"You mean, you stopped talking because you were so sad?"

"Yes. And also because I was angry. I lost my parents, and then you—well, the you I knew as a child—and then Ida, and then your mother. You know I have a bit of a temper. . . ."

Josephine nodded, remembering when he had attacked the Master.

"I was afraid if I spoke that I wouldn't be able to control myself. The day I stabbed the Master, that was the worst day of my life. I never want to hurt another person as long as I live."

Josephine could see that he meant it.

Before she could stop herself, Josephine threw her arms around her father. She hugged him fiercely. "I love you, Fargus—I mean, Father." And she did. She thought of the young Fargus she'd known, who'd been earnest and kind and good, and who'd been her true friend. And here he was with her now! She thought she would burst from happiness.

"And I love you, Josephine." He squeezed her, and when she pulled away from their embrace, she saw tears running down his cheeks. He quickly pulled out a handkerchief, wiped his face, and blew his nose. He studied her amber eyes and big eyelashes. "I wish you could see how I remember you from my childhood. You were so strong and brave and tough. I named you after that fearless girl."

Josephine tried to wrap her head around this. She had been named . . . after herself?

He smiled at her. "I can't believe that it was you—my own helpless little Josephine!"

"I'm not helpless!" she protested, pulling away.

He pulled her back and moved the hair out of her eyes. He answered contritely, "I suppose if I'd been paying better attention, I might have realized that. As a boy, the first time I saw you, I thought that you looked like my mother when she was a girl, with that big hair. You do look just like her, you know."

"I do?"

"That's why I brought you the picture of her, with her parents and all her brothers and sisters. It was the last thing she ever gave me." He dug around in his shirt pocket and brought out the photograph to show Josephine.

She looked at the girl in the middle, who she had been so sure was herself. "That girl . . . is my . . . grandmother?"

"Yes."

And as Josephine studied the photograph more closely, she could see that the girl in the picture had slightly darker hair and that her nose was just an ooch bigger than her own. She studied the rest of the picture. "Those people are all my relatives?"

"Yes."

She smiled and took the photo from her father. She placed it on a shelf above the sink, where she could see it every day. Josephine liked the idea of having a family, a past. She'd always felt so disconnected from the rest of the world. And she was an outcast in her own town.

She suddenly felt angry at Fargus and needed to tell him why. She turned and said, "Father, everyone thinks you're so mean! They hate wearing gloves, and you make them wear them anyway!" Josephine couldn't believe her own daring, but once she got started, she couldn't stop. "And they think you're greedy and rude and a snob because you never speak. And all the children hate me because of you!" The tears began again.

Mr. Russing was completely taken aback. "Why do they hate *you*? I'm the one . . . oh, what have I done?" He shook his head. "I didn't force people to wear gloves because I wanted money. I did it because . . . I was ashamed of my hand. I didn't want to explain how it got this way. To you . . . to anyone. I figured if everyone had to wear gloves, then no one would ever ask me why I was wearing them."

Josephine sniffed. "But it's still not fair."

He nodded. "I didn't realize it was affecting you. I'm sorry."

"It affects everyone in the town! Will you change the law, Father?"

"Would that make you happy?"

Josephine nodded vigorously, amazed that he would do something like that for her.

He smiled and said, "Then it's done. I'll tell the mayor tomorrow. "

That night, Josephine and her father cooked dinner together, and Josephine told him all about her adventures. She explained all about Ned, Morgan, and the claganmeter. When she told him about what she had done to Stairway Ruth and Kitchen Maggie, he burst out laughing. "That's fantastic!" he chortled. Josephine watched him in awe, never having seen him laugh before.

He stopped stirring their stew. "Can I see it?" he asked.

"What?"

"The claganmeter."

Josephine pulled the folded instrument from her pocket and handed it to him.

"Incredible," he said. "It's so simple."

"What are you going to do with it?" she asked, afraid of losing him. She thought of her mother, and her grandparents, and Ida, and all the people her father had lost. Perhaps he would use the claganmeter to go searching for them.

"Nothing," he said. "I'm not going to do anything with it. Everything I need is right here." And he handed it back to her.

She smiled, placed the claganmeter next to the family photograph, and began to set the table for two.